Books by Shirleen Davies

Historical Western Romance Series

MacLarens of Fire Mountain

Tougher than the Rest, Book One
Faster than the Rest, Book Two
Harder than the Rest, Book Three
Stronger than the Rest, Book Four
Deadlier than the Rest, Book Five
Wilder than the Rest, Book Six

Redemption Mountain

Redemption's Edge, Book One
Wildfire Creek, Book Two
Sunrise Ridge, Book Three
Dixie Moon, Book Four
Survivor Pass, Book Five

MacLarens of Boundary Mountain

Colin's Quest, Book One,
Brodie's Gamble, Book Two, Releasing 2016

Always Love You

**MacLarens of Fire Mountain
Contemporary Romance Series**

SHIRLEEN DAVIES

**Book Five in the MacLarens of Fire
Mountain**

Contemporary Romance Series

Avalanche Ranch Press, LLC
PO Box 12618
Prescott, AZ 86304

Book design and conversions by Joseph Murray at 3rdplanetpublishing.com

Cover design by The Killion Group

ISBN: 978-1-941786-14-7

I care about quality, so if you find something in error, please contact me via email at shirleen@shirleendavies.com.

Description

**Always Love You – Book Five
MacLarens of Fire Mountain
Contemporary Romance Series**

"Romance, adventure, motorcycles, cowboys, suspense—everything you want in a contemporary western romance novel."

Eric Sinclair loves his bachelor status. His work at MacLaren Enterprises leaves him with plenty of time to ride his horse as well as his Harley...and date beautiful women without a thought to commitment.

Amber Anderson is the new person at MacLaren Enterprises. Her passion for marketing landed her what she believes to be the perfect job—until she steps into her first meeting to find the man she left, but still loves, sitting at the management table—his disdain for her clear. Eric won't allow the past to taint his professional behavior, nor will he repeat his mistakes with Amber, even though love for her pulses through him as strong as ever.

As they strive to mold a working relationship, unexpected danger confronts those close to them, pitting the MacLarens and Sinclairs against an evil who stalks one member but threatens them all.

Eric can't get the memories of their passionate past out of his mind, while Amber wrestles with feelings she thought long buried. Will they be able to put the past behind them to reclaim the love lost years before?
Read, Always Love You, book five in the MacLarens of Fire Mountain Contemporary Romance series.

Dedication

This book is dedicated to all of my fellow authors who continue to offer their invaluable experience and encourage me with their amazing support. Thanks so much!

Acknowledgements

Thanks also to my editor, Deborah Gunn, proofreader, Alicia Carmical, and all of my beta readers. Their insights and suggestions are greatly appreciated.

As always, many thanks to my wonderful resources, including Diane Lebow, who has been a whiz at guiding my social media endeavors, my cover designer, Kim Killion, and Joseph Murray who is a whiz at formatting my books for both print and electronic versions.

Always Love You

Prologue

Los Angeles, California

"He's got you by the balls, my friend. Either do what is asked or your little girl will pay the consequences." The raspy, threatening voice burned through Robbie Morgan's mind. He wanted nothing more than to pull the phone from the wall and smash it on the hard, tile floor.

"Harming my daughter will do nothing to make me fall in line. Besides, what man would hurt his own granddaughter?" Robbie asked, scrubbing a hand over his two-day-old stubble.

"Sonny doesn't fit the description of a normal grandfather. He wants his son to follow him as the leader one day. All he's asking is that you send her away, let others raise her until a time when you can bring her back in a way that won't jeopardize the club."

Robbie hated the knowledge his sweet, young daughter could be a bargaining chip between rival motorcycle clubs, yet that's what she had become ever since her mother had left—on the back of a rival club member's bike. She'd relinquished all custody of their daughter to Robbie, giving up her rights. Now she wanted their daughter back and was using Robbie's love for the little girl to force a confrontation.

"To hell with him asking me. It's an order and you damn well know it. My old man doesn't understand. I'll need time to make arrangements—if I do this."

If they ran, Sonny would search until he found them, then send her away someplace where Robbie would never find her—if he lived after whatever discipline Sonny ordered.

"Oh, you'll do it. It's about respecting Sonny and the club. He's being generous. You have seventy-two hours to make this happen."

The line went dead, along with all of Robbie's plans for his beautiful, seven-year-old daughter. He slammed the receiver down, cursing a string of oaths before hearing the screen door creak open.

"Daddy! Guess what I got today?" His daughter ran up and wrapped her arms around his neck as he bent to greet her.

He swallowed the lump in his throat, accepting their time together had been sliced to a few short days. "I don't know, sugar, what?"

She pulled a little pink wallet from her backpack and held it out to him, a proud smile on her face. "This! I won the spelling bee. Isn't it the best?"

"Yes, it is the best," he choked out as his mind sorted through what needed to be done. "I have a surprise for you too, sugar."

"What?" Her excited voice told him she expected something great.

"We are taking a trip. We'll pack and leave after dinner."

"Where are we going, Daddy?"

"It's a surprise, sugar, but I'm sure you'll like it." He stood and turned from her, unable to suppress his emotions any longer.

Dinner and packing didn't take long. He knew where he needed to go, a small town in Wyoming. It would take two days by car. Two days before he'd be forced to give up his child.

******

Morning Springs, Wyoming

"Are you certain, Robbie? Once you sign these papers, it will be difficult to change things." Crystal O'Malley had grown up with Robbie Morgan in the same Los Angeles neighborhood, until her family moved when she went off to college. They'd always been close, had stayed in touch, and now he reached out to the social worker at the Department of Health and Human Services. She worked in the division handling foster care needs and adoption.

"Yes, I'm certain." Robbie looked through the glass wall separating him from his daughter, who played with another social worker, a friend of Crystal's.

"Can you tell me any more about why you're doing this? I know how much you love her. It makes no sense."

"I've told you all I can. Believe me, you don't want to know anything more about what's happening." He reached toward her, wrapping his large hand around her slender wrist. "Promise you'll find a good home for her with a family who'll love her." His voice cracked on the last words and he pulled away.

"I'll handle this personally and make certain she has a good home." Crystal's chest tightened at the pain she saw on her friend's face. At one time she'd envisioned them as a couple. Then his father had taken a path outside the law, joined an outlaw motorcycle club, and dragged Robbie with him. She'd heard Sonny had formed his owned club not long after. There'd been nothing she could do for him then. Now she could.

"Will I get to know who adopts her?"

"If they agree to an open adoption, yes, but I'm not sure that's what you want given the circumstances. You'd need to supply them your contact address, although, we could work it so everything goes through me."

"I don't know where I'll be."

"Then everything should go through me. She'll be in foster care for a period of time until we find her a home. I handle cases every day and I'm certain she won't be in the system for long." She squeezed his arm. "You have all my contact information—at work and home. I'm here for you, Robbie, anytime, no matter the hour."

Robbie nodded, unable to form a word through a throat tightened from grief.

"Are you ready to say goodbye to her?"

His gaze snapped to Crystal's, a look of pure panic in them before he shot from his chair and started for the door. "No. I can't...just tell her I had to leave...that I love her...I'll always love her."

"Robbie, wait! You can't leave her like this..."

He turned toward her, tears filling his eyes, shook his head once and disappeared out the door.

Chapter One

Denver, Colorado

December, 20 years later...

"How many more?" Jace MacLaren peered out the window toward the nearby mountains already covered in snow as another storm threatened.

"One." Heath MacLaren passed a résumé across the table to his brother.

They'd interviewed three of four candidates in the last six hours and wanted to get the decision finalized. It had taken three months to get this far, reviewing over forty résumés, completing telephone interviews with twelve before identifying four who possessed all the requirements. One would be hired today to become the director of their new marketing group. The search had been communicated to MacLaren board members and no one else.

They'd chosen Denver for final interviews, which would enable them to keep the position quiet as long as possible. Heath expected to announce the establishment of a marketing department and the hiring of a director at Christmas, a few days before Kade and Brooke's wedding.

Jace scanned the résumé. "Works in Denver after spending a few years in New York. Glowing references. Attended college in California, finished a marketing degree in New York, and is enrolled in an online master's program." He glanced up at Heath. "Volunteer assistant coach for a local lacrosse team and volunteers with foster children. Interesting."

The MacLaren Foundation focused on services and programs for foster youth. Heath and Jace were two of the board members.

"All of the candidates today have the education and experience. We need to find the one person who will work the best with the team. Brooke has done an exceptional job so far, and we both know Cam and Eric are indispensable. I'm certain we'll be equally impressed with Kade. The right person must fit with them all." Heath glanced up from the résumé. "And us."

"As of right now, my vote is for the second one we met today," Jace said.

"Agreed."

They turned at a knock on the door before it swung open.

"Your two o'clock is here." Phyllis Jurgensen, Heath and Jace's assistant, had traveled with them to Denver. She'd become as essential as any one of the management team members. Plus, she knew all the personalities involved in the family owned company.

"I'll be right there." Jace stood and walked toward the door. "Let's wrap this up and get home." He disappeared into the hallway, entering the reception area as a striking woman, hair falling loose around her shoulders, wearing a conservative gray suit, stood to greet him.

Jace extended his hand. "Miss Anderson, I'm Jace MacLaren."

"It's a pleasure, Mr. MacLaren."

"Please, follow me and we'll get started." Jace opened the door to the conference room, letting her enter first.

Heath stepped around the table. "Good afternoon, Miss Anderson. I'm Heath MacLaren. It's good to meet you."

They'd expected the interview to last an hour. After two, Heath signaled an end to the meeting, walked her to the elevators, then returned to see a broad smile on Jace's face.

"What do you think?" Heath asked.

"Impressive. Excellent experience, great answers, professional, and a sense of humor—"

"Which is a necessity."

"How do you compare her to the others?" Jace asked.

"Miss Anderson, hands down."

"I'll let Phyllis know to finish the background check and prepare an offer."

As had become their habit, Jace wrote down a number on a piece of paper and slid it across the table.

"Plus bonus," Heath said. "We want her in Fire Mountain by early February."

******

Fire Mountain, Arizona

February

"When do you expect to wrap it up and return?" Heath spoke on the phone with his stepson, Eric Sinclair, director of their land acquisition and development division. He'd been in Austin for the last week, visiting possible locations for another office complex. They'd just finished reviewing his recommendations.

"Unless you have an objection, I thought I'd stay the weekend, look at the top two choices once more, then be available to attend some big deal supper hosted by the real estate broker we're using."

"Business and pleasure, I presume."

"Absolutely," Eric chuckled. He'd been traveling nonstop for the last few weeks, visiting three states and countless parcels of undeveloped land. He'd taken one day off.

"I'll set up a meeting for Monday to introduce the latest member of the management team."

"No problem. I'll fly in late Sunday."

"Stop by the house if it's not too late." Heath hung up, knowing his wife, Annie, would want to see her son after such an extended absence. He looked up as Phyllis opened his door.

"Miss Anderson is here to see you."

"Have her come in." Heath set aside Eric's report and stood, exchanging greetings, and offering her a chair. "I hear you've found a place."

"Miss Jurgensen is the one who found it for me. Someone she knows had a vacancy in their complex. I moved in this weekend." Amber

Anderson straightened her skirt and glanced around the spacious office. "I hope it was all right that I stopped by unexpected."

"Glad you did. I'm setting up a meeting Monday morning to introduce you and go over the basics of the new department. I want you to meet the rest of the management team, then set up meetings with each one over the next week. Have you had a chance to review the current marketing material?"

"I have." Amber reached into her bag to pull out a folder. "I hope you don't mind, but I've jotted down some thoughts." She handed a typed memo to Heath, who scanned it, his face indicating nothing of his thoughts.

"This is a good start. I'm certain you'll identify more areas for improvement as you meet with the management team." He slipped the memo into his desk. "I'll have Phyllis arrange for lunch on Monday with Jace and the president of our Cold Creek, Colorado group. Our brother, Rafe, won't be in Fire Mountain for another week. You'll need to meet with him as he heads up our bull bucking stock company in Montana."

"The way I understand it, each department or separate company handles all their own marketing, correct?" Amber asked.

"Correct. We want to build continuity into the program, do some cross marketing, and try to build on each other's strengths. Right now we're duplicating efforts. We need a more efficient and effective system."

"All right. I guess I'd better let you get back to work. Thanks again for letting me stop in." Amber grabbed her bag and slipped it over her shoulder. "I'll look forward to meeting everyone on Monday."

******

Austin, Texas

"Eric." Keith Vance, a partner in the commercial real estate company giving the party, motioned him over. "There's someone I'd like you to meet."

"Jax Perry, this is Eric Sinclair. His company is the one I've been telling you about. Jax's company handles all of our marketing, plus works with several development firms. Excuse me while I say hello to someone." Keith walked off, leaving the two alone.

Eric let his gaze wander over the stunning beauty. Tall and slender, she had an almost exotic air about her in a black, tight-fitting short skirt, low-cut royal blue silk blouse, which matched her eyes, and jet-black hair pulled back at the knap with a silver clasp. Her skin seemed translucent, like a glazed piece of ivory colored porcelain.

"Keith tells me he's been running you all over the city to look at land." Jax sipped her martini, watching him over the rim of her glass. Her body's response to Eric had been immediate and intense.

"Running is a good description. He had two pages of properties, plus the pertinent data on each. It took two days to pare it down to four." He couldn't seem to look away. "Would you care to dance?"

"I'd love to." Jax set her glass down and walked with Eric onto the dance floor. She couldn't recall the last time she'd wanted to grab a man's hand and walk out right then and there, find the nearest bed and spend all night in it. She guessed herself to be three or four years older, which worked well for her—great looking guy, good times, no strings.

They danced twice before returning to pick up their drinks and find a table.

"Is this your first trip to Austin?"

"It is. Most of my time is spent between our headquarters in Arizona, plus sites in Colorado,

Utah, and Montana. We've made the decision to include Texas in our plans." Eric watched her cross her long legs and worked to control his response to her. He noticed she didn't wear stockings even though the nights had turned chilly and the party was held outside. "Have you lived here long?"

"I'm a native, although I did attend college in Florida. I worked in Miami, then Dallas before returning home. I've known Keith since high school. He's the one who suggested I return and start using my marketing skills to help others. His wife and I have been friends for years. Where are you from?"

"Born and raised in California. I moved to Arizona to accept the position with MacLaren Enterprises." He looked around for anyone who might be looking for her. "Are you married, Jax?"

Her throaty laugh filled the air. "No. And you?"

"Single as they come." Eric could already tell where this was headed. He had to make a decision soon whether to go with whatever happened or spend another night in his hotel room, alone.

"Tell me what you've seen so far? Have you found what you're looking for?"

Something about her stare told him she wasn't talking about land.

"Possibly." He nursed a gin and tonic, a habit he'd gotten into when attending social events. One drink could last him all night.

Other than a brief relationship months before, he preferred an occasional liaison, making certain the woman knew nothing would come from it.

He'd been foolish when younger, giving his heart to his high school sweetheart and making plans during his junior year of college to marry after they both graduated. She'd walked out with little hesitation when offered an opportunity out of state. His whole world had slipped away when she left, bruising not just his heart, but his self-respect and confidence. It had taken his roommates months to get him out of the apartment they shared and longer to date. In retrospect, they weren't so much dates as they were hook-ups—a pattern he preferred even years later.

"Why don't we go somewhere a little more private and talk about what you've seen? Perhaps I can help you sort through the options and come to a decision." Jax's mouth curved into a slight, knowing smile. She'd watched him check her out, more than once, her instincts screaming they would both be open to spending time together—such as one steamy night.

Eric swirled the drink and then brought it to his lips, finishing it in one swallow before setting it on a nearby table. "I'll follow you."

Chapter Two

Fire Mountain

"Welcome back." Annie MacLaren hugged Brooke and Kade, who'd just returned from their honeymoon in San Diego. "You don't have to tell me how much fun you had, I can see it on your faces."

"It couldn't have been better." Brooke laced her arm through her mother's. "I'm glad we took the full month. I think we should do it often."

"Agreed. Every time we get married," Kade joked, grabbing their bags and heading toward the car. "How's everyone here?"

"Good. Eric is checking on some property in Texas and will be back tomorrow. Cam and Lainey will return from Cold Creek late tonight, and Cassie is settling into her training role at the office. Same old stuff." Annie slid into the driver's seat. "How about a stop at the ranch house before you head home?"

"Sounds good." Kade draped an arm over Brooke's shoulder, pulling her close.

"Rafe is supposed to be here next weekend." Annie wanted to give Kade a heads-up his father would be in town, staying with her and Heath. A father he knew of but had never met until a few months before. They were working on building a relationship and each visit showed progress. Although Kade occasionally used his birth surname of MacLaren, most of the time he still preferred Taylor, the name his mother had taken after his birth. Perhaps in time Kade would be able to let go of the resentment he still felt when he saw Rafe. He didn't believe there was any way he'd ever be able to call him father as Rafe wanted.

"Is there something special he's coming in for?" Brooke asked. She'd been supportive of both Rafe and Kade, hoping they'd someday find common ground and her husband would embrace the love his father offered. She also hoped Kade could build relationships with his stepbrothers and stepsisters, who'd all made the trip to attend their wedding. The oldest, Mitch, had recently moved to Fire Mountain to work at the headquarters for several months to learn the business.

"A board meeting, plus Heath and Jace want him to meet the newest member of the staff."

"The new marketing director?" Kade looked forward to meeting the new man on the team.

"Yes. Apparently she's found a place to live and you'll all meet her on Monday." Annie turned into the long drive signaling the entrance to the ranch.

"A woman?" Kade asked.

Brooke turned to glare at him. "Something wrong with that?" With a Ph.D. in management systems, she could've been offered a job with numerous private companies, as well as a teaching post at several colleges. She'd elected to go with Heath and Jace's offer, and until the new hire, had been the sole female on the management team. Another woman was welcome news.

"Nope. Just surprised. Not too many women have the experience Jace said they wanted. I don't have to tell you how specialized their businesses are and how few people understand what's needed. I watched Jace toss aside one résumé after another as he poured over them a few months back. I'm just glad they found someone."

"Heath said the same. They got it down to four and she was the lone woman." Annie came to a stop in the wide parking area in front of the house.

"Have you met her?" Brooke asked.

"I don't know her name or anything else about her. Of course, I haven't asked. They've always done a fine job without my interference."

******

"I still can't believe I landed the job." Amber held the phone between her shoulder and ear while preparing a salad between sips of white wine. "It's a dream position."

"Don't rub it in." Dana, Amber's closest friend, still worked at the same company in Denver where they'd met. She'd grown up in a small town in Wyoming, leaving to attend college north of Denver. She knew every inch of the sprawling city. Her graphics design job and Amber's in marketing brought them together during Dana's first week, a few months after Amber started. Both were single and on the fast track.

"I know you love Denver, but I'm going to keep my eyes and ears open for possibilities out here. You've never seen this part of Arizona and it's nothing like you'd expect." Amber popped a crouton in her mouth and grabbed a fork, not bothering to put the salad in a smaller bowl. She'd power it down in one sitting.

"Perhaps I should come out for a visit. I've got over a week's vacation coming." Dana switched screens on her computer to her calendar. "Maybe in March."

"Let me get settled, earn some time off myself, then definitely. Be prepared, though. You're going to want to stay once you see Fire Mountain. I wish I could've been there to help with your move into the new apartment. Timing couldn't have been worse."

"Don't worry about it. An opening came up in a new complex in downtown Denver and I jumped on it. I hired a truck and a couple of the guys in the sales department helped me move. I think I was out of the old place before any of the neighbors realized I was gone. And it's got space enough for my car and bike."

"Sounds perfect. Don't forget to text me your new address," Amber reminded her.

"Will do. Now, tell me who you've met so far. Anyone fascinating?"

"Not unless you count the buff Marine who lives below me, handles security for a company in town, and drives a hot sports car." Amber dumped the remnants of her salad into the sink, poured another glass of wine, and settled onto the sofa.

"Wow! Sounds promising."

"He's fifty-one and married."

"Oh." Dana's deflated voice made Amber smile. "Isn't that just the way of it? Neither of us have had anyone special since...well, since..."

"It's all right, you can say it. Years. It's been years since either of us has had more than a couple dull experiences with mediocre outcomes, but I believe my life is about to change. I can sense something big will happen to me now that I've made this move."

Dana's voice quieted, becoming thoughtful. "Do you still think about him? And don't ask who."

"Sure I do. I wonder what he's doing, where he lives, if he ever got married. None of the wondering does me a bit of good. He answers my two emails a year with one short sentence, if I'm lucky. You'd think if someone took the time to wish him a happy birthday and Christmas greetings, he'd at least share some information, but nothing. Well, I'm through trying to reach out."

"I sense a new Amber is ready to emerge. It's about time." Dana wasn't much better. She'd had a couple of casual relationships in the years since her boyfriend met someone new and moved out of the apartment they shared.

"There's something about this place, as if it holds possibilities for me beyond what I'd expected. I know the new job is most of it, but I believe the move has helped pull me from the disillusionment I've carried for too long. It's time to move on and be open to new opportunities."

"You mean new men," Dana prompted.

"I mean new people—new friends and experiences. Well, it's getting late and I have some reading to do before my first day. Wish me luck."

"Always. Sleep well."

******

"Tell him to come into the board room as soon as he arrives." Heath hung up the phone then turned to the others. "Eric's plane landed. He'll be here in about five minutes. I'll bring in the newest employee once he arrives."

"Are you going to tell us about her or make us wait?" Cameron Sinclair asked. The oldest of Annie Sinclair MacLaren's children, Cam was the president of their bucking bronc stock company in Colorado.

Heath took a few minutes to provide the essentials—her experience, education, reasons for leaving her last job, ending as the door opened and Eric walked in.

"Apologies. Last night's plane was cancelled and the one this morning was delayed for weather." He nodded at everyone and took a seat next to his sister, Brooke. "Did I miss anything?"

"A review of the new employee's background. I won't repeat it, so you'll need to get it from her yourself." Heath hit the intercom. "Phyllis, please send her in."

The conversations continued around the table for a few minutes before the door opened. Heads turned to see a striking young woman walk into the room. She smiled at Heath and Jace, then let her gaze move from one person to the next until the brilliant smile she'd first worn faded as she landed on one person.

Heath stood. "Everyone, this is—"

"Amber!" Brooke pushed from her chair and almost ran to wrap her arms around the friend she'd lost contact with years before. "You're the new hire?" She pulled back, then the full impact of what was happening hit her. "Oh my..." She turned her head to the others.

Cam stood and walked around the table, giving Amber a hug. "It's been a long time."

"Hello, Cam. Yes, it has." The perfect job had turned into the perfect nightmare in the span of a few seconds.

Heath cocked an eyebrow and looked at Jace, whose blank stare indicated the confusion he felt.

"I'm guessing you know my stepson, Cam, and stepdaughter, Brooke." Heath's eyes narrowed on Amber.

"Uh...yes, sir. I've known the Sinclair family for several years, however, we lost touch when I moved from California to New York." She summoned her courage and looked at Eric, this time holding his gaze and deciding the best approach would be to hold her ground. She could see his jaw work, the beautiful golden brown eyes she remembered glaring at her with what she guessed to be total contempt. "I didn't realize the Sinclair's were part of the business or I would've mentioned it to you."

"Then you must know my stepson, Eric, as well." Heath walked toward her, stopping next to Eric's chair.

The pain in her chest felt like a vice, squeezing until she couldn't breathe. She tried to suck in air and remain calm. She needed this job, wanted it, and no prior life mistake would cause her to lose it.

"Yes, I know Eric."

Heath glanced at Jace, then back at Brooke. "I'd like to make a suggestion. If everyone will excuse us for a few minutes, I want to speak with Eric, Jace, and Amber. We'll resume the meeting in a few minutes."

Amber found she couldn't seem to move as if she were anchored in place, held tight by some invisible force. She waited until the others had filed out, Brooke giving her an encouraging look as she passed. The sound of the door closing jolted her into looking up.

"Amber, why don't you have a seat here?" Heath motioned to a chair next to him, across from Eric and Jace.

She nodded and let him pull out the chair, an old school, gentlemanly habit, which she welcomed. "Thank you." Her hands automatically stilled in her lap, her fingers laced, almost painfully.

Heath looked at Eric. "You have yet to say anything, Eric. If there's something you want to get off your chest, I'd suggest now is the time."

******

Eric's weekend had gone better than planned. His night with Jax pulled him from his recent pattern of takeout meals, dinner meetings, and long days. She'd been fun and everything he'd thought when he'd made the decision to follow her home. He hadn't intended to spend the night, but her relaxed manner, sense of humor, and no strings attitude made him feel connected, if just for one night.

He'd left her house Sunday morning after breakfast to meet Keith and visit the two best sites, not making any plans to see her again. If they ran into each other, fine, although he did invite her to contact him if she were ever in Fire Mountain.

Eric's Sunday night flight had been cancelled and the first plane on Monday delayed by weather. He'd called Heath, then sat back and relaxed in the High Flyers club, rehashing the night with Jax, a smile playing across his face. He'd kept in good humor all through the flight home, feeling the normal stress melt away. Now this.

He'd done a double take when Amber walked into the room. When Brooke jumped up and hugged her, he knew his vision hadn't betrayed him. His ex-fiancée, the woman who'd sucked the life from him when she'd left for New York, stood at the head of the table, looking more stunningly beautiful than he remembered.

And the punch of it was, his body responded instantly, as if all the years they'd been apart hadn't happened. As if she hadn't ripped his heart from his chest, leaving an open gap which never healed.

Of all the people Heath and Jace could've hired, it had to be Amber Anderson. And she'd be his peer, someone he'd see each time he worked in the office, at staff meetings, and during company events. Could he deal with it and not let the past affect him? He honestly didn't know.

He leaned forward, resting his arms on the table and clasping his hands before clearing his throat.

"Amber and I planned to marry before she left for New York. We haven't seen each other since. To be honest, I don't know how to react, or even what to say."

So this was Amber, Heath thought. Of course it had never come up during the interviews or background check. She wouldn't know Eric Sinclair lived in Fire Mountain, held a position as a director at MacLaren Enterprises, and was Heath's stepson.

"It appears we have a dilemma. We need to figure out if it can be solved, which means consensus from all four of us." He shot a pointed look at Eric then Amber. "You need to know, Amber, Eric is vital to the future of MacLaren Enterprises. He's done an outstanding job and we can't afford to lose him."

Amber nodded, knowing no matter how much she wanted this job, she had to find a way to graciously exit. No one would win if she held tight to a position where she couldn't succeed.

"I understand, Heath. It's been a pleasure meeting you and Jace. Perhaps in the future, if the situation changes..." She glanced at her hands, then back up at Heath as she started to rise. "Well, I suppose I should—"

"Perhaps I wasn't clear," Heath interrupted. "We reviewed a truckload of résumés, interviewed four outstanding people, and offered you the job. You got it because you have the skills, background, personality, and drive to succeed at MacLaren. You just need to know that Eric isn't going anywhere, so the burden of making this situation work may fall more on you than on him. It may not seem fair, but that's the way it has to be."

"You...you still want me to stay?" She could feel her bottom lip quiver and worked to control it, lest someone notice.

"Eric must agree as you'll be forced to work together, sometimes long nights, long weekends, whatever it takes to get your jobs done." He looked at Eric. "I need to know if you can do this."

Eric had seen her bottom lip tremble. No one else would ever notice it, but Eric did, having been around her many times when she'd been dealt bad news or feared something. It used to be he could put an arm around her, draw her close, and love the uncertainty away. She'd do all she could to hide it, but deep down, he knew she was scared. This job meant a lot to her. If he balked, said he couldn't work with her, it would be like kicking a puppy.

He sat back in his chair and folded his arms across his chest. "If she can do the job, handle everything the two of you throw at her, then I have no problem with it."

Amber's eyes widened in surprise. Never would she have expected Eric to agree.

"Amber, can you do the job given the past?" Heath looked at her.

"Yes, sir. I can do the job."

"Fine. Jace, please notify the others and we'll get this meeting started."

Chapter Three

Eric returned to his office, mumbling a curse as he slammed the notebook on his desk, and ran a hand through his dark blond hair. Amber Anderson. The meeting had lasted over an hour, each moment feeling as if a knife had been plunged into his chest. He thought the feelings he had for her died years ago. He'd built a new life, had a job he loved, dated whomever he chose, traveled, and had no expectations of falling for someone anytime soon—maybe never again.

His world had been torn apart, once more, when she walked into the room. Now he had to learn to deal with her presence and the real kicker—the renewed pull he felt toward her. Life could be a real pain sometimes. He grabbed his ringing phone, not looking at the caller ID.

"Yeah."

"It's Kade. Are you back in your office?"

Eric let out a breath and closed his eyes. "I'm here. You need something?"

"I have one more meeting, then I'm done. Cam, Mitch, and I will come by to get you."

"For what?" Eric pinched the bridge of his nose between his thumb and forefinger.

"We're going out. No arguments. Steak and whatever else you want. Plan on it." Kade hung up without waiting for an answer.

Eric would've laughed if his stomach wasn't in a knot the size of a watermelon. He'd penciled in a meeting with Amber at eight the next morning to bring her up to speed on his current and future projects. They'd talk about what had worked in the past and what he wanted to see for marketing in his department going forward. Just two colleagues on their best, professional behavior.

"Ah, hell," he hissed before dropping into his chair and resting his head in his hands.

******

Amber looked up at the sound of a knock on her door. "Yes?"

Brooke pushed the door open. "May I come in?"

"Of course." Amber set aside the papers she'd been reviewing in preparation for her meetings with Eric and Cam tomorrow. She didn't know what to expect from either of the Sinclair men. One she'd once loved with all her heart and the other she'd always seen as a big brother. "Oh, sorry." Amber picked up the stacks of folders piled high on both guest chairs. "It seems the marketing manager had file cabinets full of information. Mostly useless."

Brooke took a seat and looked around, remembering her first day at MacLaren Enterprises. She felt overwhelmed and somewhat intimidated. Amber faced an even bigger obstacle in Eric.

"I know you're swamped, getting ready for a big week, but I wondered if you might be able to have dinner with me. We have so much to catch up on."

Amber's first instinct was to decline. She did have a lot to review in preparation for her meetings and needed to come across strong. Her stomach elected that moment to let loose with a growl even Brooke couldn't miss.

"I guess we have our answer. Is Italian all right or would you prefer something else?"

"Italian sounds good. What time?" Amber rested her hip against the edge of the desk.

"How about I stop by in an hour. Will that give you enough time?" Brooke asked.

"I'll be ready." Amber watched Brooke leave, closing the door behind her as she greeted someone in the hallway. She'd been surprised at the cordial and relaxed atmosphere within minutes of arriving this morning. It didn't take more than this one day to realize the friendliness belied a strong work ethic and commitment to results.

Amber reached for the folder she'd tossed down when Brooke entered and began to read. After three attempts to finish the first page, she dropped it and stood, walking to the window with a view to the mountains. She hoped to find time to hike, do some camping, maybe buy another motorcycle and visit the Grand Canyon—assuming she stayed employed long enough.

Eric had taken a giant step by not blocking her employment. He could've scuttled it with a few well-chosen words. Instead, he'd taken the professional path of showing Heath and Jace how he could be a team player, no matter the personal issues of his decision.

She couldn't read anything into his action, such as extending an olive branch to her. He would be more likely to show it to her then break it in half. She knew the pain her decision to leave for New York caused him. What he didn't know was how his attitude toward her request—his absolute refusal to discuss it—tortured her just as much. He may not love her any longer, or even like her, but he'd tolerate her for the sake of his job.

He'd attempted to hide the way he watched her during the meeting. Most in the room wouldn't have noticed his gaze shifting to Amber every couple of minutes and holding. She did. At first she felt uncomfortable and tried to shift away, then decided to roll with it as she did when any colleague became curious about another. She'd let the shock pass, settle into her job, and excel, as she'd always done.

******

"Tell me about Kade." Amber sipped her after dinner coffee, trying to relax for the meetings tomorrow with Eric and Cam. She had a sense both could be difficult, almost as if she were questioning a hostile witness in a courtroom. Of course, she may be reading too much into the situation.

"Not until you tell me about you and Eric. We've spent the entire evening talking about my time at the university, my job, your past jobs, and nerves about your new one. It's time you gave me the details of what happened between the two of you." Brooke settled back in her seat and crossed her legs, ignoring her friend's discomfort.

Amber blew out a slow breath. "It's been so long."

"Do you still care for him?"

"I'm not in love with him anymore, if that's what you're asking." She took another sip of coffee and laid down her cup. "It's my fault we split. I wanted to try an opportunity in New York. All I asked Eric for was six months to give it a shot. He refused to talk about it, told me I needed to choose between him and leaving. I was naïve. I thought he'd come to his senses and follow me east. Instead, he helped me load my clothes, waved goodbye, and that's the last I saw of him until this morning. I was young, impulsive, and angry—not a good combination to make a decision such as breaking an engagement. If I could go back in time, have a do-over..." her wistful voice trailed off as she remembered the tears in her eyes when she'd driven away.

"What would you do?"

She picked up her cup and rolled it between her hands. "I should've stayed longer, until he'd grown used to the idea, then tried to get him to talk. His face turned to stone when I first brought it up. He didn't even ask why it mattered so much to me or would I consider waiting until the end of the year, or maybe both of us flying east to check it out. Nothing. Just a flat refusal to discuss it. Looking back, I think I just needed him to talk it through with me."

"You were both so young. They say everything happens for a reason. Maybe the split will prove to be the best decision you've ever made."

"If you're implying we'll fall in love again, you might as well put the thought out of your head. When I left, the potential for a future with him vanished. I've come to accept I no longer matter to him and he's not the man for me. He's moved on and so have I." She made the decision to ask what she'd wanted to all night. "Has he ever married?"

"From what I know, he's come nowhere close. Don't get me wrong, Eric is no celibate monk. He dates, has a great time, then splits before anything can develop. It's as if he intentionally builds a wall between him and any woman who might threaten his bachelor status. If he ever does marry, I'm guessing it will be a long time after he's become an uncle several times over. What about you? You ever come close?"

"Just with Eric."

Something about Amber's response tore at Brooke's heart. She believed Amber handled the last years in a much different way than Eric. "Do you date, go out at all?"

"I've dated over the years. No one special. I can't even remember the last time I had...well, you know." She glanced at an older couple who walked in holding hands then shifted in her chair. "Anyway, it's been a while. I've decided once I get settled in my job, I'm going to make a stronger effort to meet new people and date." Amber looked at her watch. "Guess I'd better get going. Big day tomorrow. Don't forget you're on the calendar for Wednesday."

Brooke stood by her car, watching as Amber drove off. Much of what she said made sense, although she couldn't shake the feeling Amber might be kidding herself, the same as Brooke believed Eric had been doing for years. Fate had thrown them back together, and she feared both had a rough ride ahead of them.

******

"Last one, then I'm out of here." Eric licked salt from the rim of the glass, tossed back the tequila, then sucked on a lime. He shook his head, trying to clear it from the third shot he'd had in less than an hour. He'd had a gin and tonic before dinner and a couple of glasses of wine with his steak. Probably not the best choices given the way his day had gone.

"What are you going to do about Amber?" Cam signaled the waitress for a round of coffee.

Eric knew there was no sense avoiding the discussion. "Hell, I don't know."

"That bad, huh?" Kade asked.

"You know how you feel about Brooke?"

"Yeah."

"I felt the same about Amber. It never once occurred to me she didn't feel the same. It took a long time to get over my anger at the way she left."

"Do you still love her?" Mitch asked.

Eric cradled his coffee cup between both hands and looked up. "Not a bit. I cured myself of her a long time ago. But, I'm not blind. She's turned into a beautiful woman. Just because I don't want her doesn't mean I'm oblivious to her charms."

"You do know of course, if your feelings change, there could be a few complications," Cam said.

"Of course I know, and believe me, I won't change my mind. Even if she is stunning, I have no interest in her whatsoever. That train left the station years ago." *With my heart on it*, Eric thought as he lifted his cup.

******

"Of all the men in the whole world, he has to work at MacLaren Enterprises." Dana's incredulous tone said it all.

"And he's the stepson of Heath MacLaren," Amber threw out.

"Of course he is." Sarcasm dripped from her friend's voice, and despite herself, Amber's mouth tipped up a bit. "Which means you'll have to work harder, faster, and do a better job so he can't undermine your efforts."

"I don't believe he'd—"

"Don't even go there, Amber. You may not realize it, but you just walked into a war. You're one commander and Eric is the other. You have to be prepared to outflank him at every opportunity."

This time Amber chuckled at her friend's wording. Dana had grown up in a military family, her father career Army, her mother an Army nurse, and her brothers in Special Forces. When things got tough, old sayings died hard.

"All right, I'll concede he has reasons for wanting me out of the company. You should have seen the people at the meeting. There were MacLarens and Sinclairs at almost every seat. A couple other outsiders like me, but we're a definite minority." She fell back against her pillow and took a breath. "Except, it appears all views are welcome and no one takes sides. Each person expressed their thoughts to Heath and Jace without a hint of repercussion. Maybe I'm seeing a boogie man where there isn't one."

"I'd err on the side of caution. Believe in a boogie man until you're certain no such creature exists. But you know me, I can be a little more cynical than you."

Amber could hear Dana munch into a chocolate bar with nuts, her every night snack. She'd never understood how her friend could sleep after eating almost three ounces of chocolate a few minutes before turning out the light.

"Sounds like you're ready to call it a night, and so am I. Where will you be this weekend?" Amber asked.

"Going snowboarding in Breckenridge with a few people from the office. Leave Friday night and return Sunday late afternoon. Call me, anytime, with updates. And if you need me, I'll be on the first plane out."

Amber already knew her friend would be there for her no matter what. "I'll talk to you soon. Have a good week." She set her phone aside and turned off the light, settling into new Egyptian cotton sheets, a present to herself for landing the MacLaren job.

She stared at the ceiling, listening to the sound of the clock tripping over each minute, and a drippy water faucet in the bathroom. She'd have to remember to call maintenance the next morning before work. The eight o'clock meeting with Eric would give her a couple of hours to review what she'd been given on the land acquisition and development department, which he headed.

The marketing material was pathetic, even as the success of his work guaranteed he'd be with the company a long time. Amber knew her skill in developing material and programs would enhance his already stellar performance. She needed to be able to communicate it tomorrow without appearing pushy.

As her eyes drifted shut, an image of Eric laughing and tossing her a volleyball on the beach raced across her mind. She clasped the blanket close to her chest as it tightened at the memory. Given time, the pain would pass, as it always did.

Chapter Four

"Come in," Eric called at the rap on his office door. He'd kept the blinds closed and lights off since coming in at seven. He'd toyed with downing a shot of whisky, then thought better of it. The last thing he needed was for Amber to smell liquor on his breath.

"Good morning." Amber walked in, stopping at the lack of light. Her hand moved to the switch. "Would you mind—?"

"Yes, actually, I would. Unless it's too dark for you to see." He squinted at her, trying to calm his rolling stomach and focus at the same time.

Amber bit her lower lip in an attempt to suppress a grin, recognizing a hangover when she saw one. "No, this is fine." She took a seat across from him and opened a notebook. "How would you like to start?"

His narrowed gaze focused on her as he waved a hand. "Wherever you'd like."

"All right. I thought we could review the last two major campaigns, discuss what worked and what didn't, then move to your current projects."

"Fine," he ground out as a wave of nausea hit him. He didn't know what to make of it. He'd drank a lot more in the past than he had last night and never experienced a hangover this powerful. It seemed the fates were against him this week.

An hour passed with Eric adding his input, agreeing with some of her comments and trashing others before Amber sat back in her chair. She watched as a light sheen of sweat built across his brows and he rubbed it away with his fingers. It must have been some night, she thought, and wondered if he'd spent it with a woman or at home alone, regretting he hadn't given her the boot when he had the chance.

"I believe I have enough to put some ideas together for you."

"For which properties?"

"The Utah property and the potential site in Austin is where I'd start. You said Heath and Jace tentatively approved the deal, so we might as well include it. Unless you have a different idea." She kept her tone even, professional, and courteous.

"Those two are fine."

"I'm meeting with everyone else this week and Rafe on Monday. How about we set up a time to review ideas a week from Thursday?"

He opened his calendar. "No can do. I'm in Austin again. The first of the following week is good."

"Monday morning, ten o'clock?"

He typed it in and sat back, glancing at his watch. "If that's all…"

Amber picked up her notebook and headed for the door, then turned back toward him. "And thanks."

"For what?" His face remained neutral.

"Not objecting to me joining the company."

He leaned forward, fixing her with a steady gaze. "Makes no difference to me one way or the other. If you have the skills, then it will work out. If not, you'll be gone. Simple." He turned his attention to his computer screen, dismissing her.

"Right." She closed the door, absorbing his words. At least he hadn't changed in one aspect—you could count on Eric to be direct.

He reached into his bottom drawer and pulled out a bottle of pain killers, popped two in his mouth, and washed them down with a gulp of water. His head had pounded through the entire meeting, at one point getting so bad he'd almost grabbed the bottle of aspirin while

Amber watched. He sure as hell didn't need her to think he'd gone through their entire meeting with a hangover—although true. The last shooter had sealed his fate. Now he had to get through the rest of the day, head home, and crash.

******

"You still here?" Brooke poked her head into Amber's office to find her still pouring over notes from today's meetings.

"What time is it?" Amber leaned back, stretching her arms above her head.

"Almost seven. Pack it up and I'll walk out with you."

"Kade's not here?"

"He and Jace are out of town looking at some mares for our breeding program. I don't expect him until Thursday. You feel like Chinese takeout?"

"Anything so I don't have to go to the apartment and eat cereal." Amber closed her briefcase, turned off the lights, and followed Brooke outside, noting the light still on in Eric's office. "Does he work late every night?" She nodded toward his door as they passed.

"When he's in town. Sometimes he doesn't roll in until late morning. I try not to keep up

48

with his strange schedule. Follow me and I'll show you the best Chinese restaurant in town." Brooke slid into her red SUV and took off, Amber close behind.

A mile from the office complex they passed a convenience center, the parking lot packed with choppers and people in leathers milling about. Brooke made a mental note to mention it to Kade. His past life as a DEA Special Agent had left them with some loose ends and she still felt a chill at the sight of bikers anywhere in Fire Mountain.

"Did you see those bikes?" Amber asked after they'd ordered and taken seats. "Some of them were amazing."

"You could tell from driving by them at night?"

"A few were under the lights. I'd love to take a closer look sometime."

"Do you ride?"

"I sold mine before leaving Denver. Now I wish I'd kept it. Guess I'll need to check out what's available in town, see if there's a place selling used bikes."

She'd always been fascinated by them, although she could never explain the attraction to her parents. When she moved to Denver and met Dana, her interest sparked again. Dana owned a bike during high school in Wyoming, selling it to buy a larger one when she went to college. She'd brought it to Denver and rode with a local group at least one weekend a month, cracking Amber's last bit of resistance.

Amber bought a small bike, got her license, then plunked down the money for a larger motorcycle, which she rode with Dana and her friends.

"You know Kade, Mitch, and Eric have bikes. Mitch bought one when he moved from Montana after Christmas."

Amber shifted toward Brooke, her eyes wide. "I didn't know that. Do they ride often?"

"Eric and Mitch ride their bikes to work much of the time. Kade has the most experience. All three try to ride on weekends."

"Okay, it's time you tell me more about Kade."

"You already know some of it and how we met. Kade used to ride with one of the worst motorcycle clubs in the country as part of his DEA work. He won't tell me much of what went on, just bits and pieces, but from what I do know, they're into some bad stuff."

"Here you go."

They looked up at the young waitress who handed them their bags of takeout. Amber glanced at the girl then at Brooke.

"Is it all right if we go ahead and eat here?" she asked, wanting to hear more about Kade's experiences. "If that's all right with you, Brooke."

"Of course. I'm starving."

They dug in, each taking several bites before Amber broke the silence. "Tell me more about what Kade did."

Brooke spoke of his time in Special Ops and transition to the DEA. She knew little of what he did during his undercover assignments, except the work impacted him more than he'd let on.

"There's still one case hanging out there which still bothers me."

"Which one?" Amber asked.

"His last undercover assignment with the motorcycle club. They arrested the founder and national president, plus a handful of his top people, and based on Kade's testimony, the DEA is certain they'll go to prison. The gang remains in existence with the son taking on the national president role. He's been in the number two spot for a long time and, according to Kade, has been waiting for his father to step aside."

"The father going to jail accomplished that."

"True. According to what Kade's been able to learn, the son had put a reward out for him."

Amber's chopsticks stopped midway to her mouth. "You mean like a hit?"

"I believe so. Kade is still connected with the DEA because of the case, and they keep him in the loop on anything that impacts him. I overheard him talking with J.D. Montalban, a DEA agent who was pulled from another assignment to keep tabs on the gang. He's the one who warned Kade of the threat." Brooke shrugged, trying not to seem alarmed.

"When did he learn this?" Amber asked.

"On Sunday."

"The day after you got home from your honeymoon. Great timing." Amber's brow furrowed as she absorbed what Brooke had told her. "What does he plan to do?"

"He's alerted Heath, Jace, Cam, Mitch, and Eric, plus everyone who works around the ranch house. He's also notified the police chief and sheriff. They were both involved in what happened last summer. The DEA is trying to learn what they can to substantiate the threat. Until they do, their hands are tied as far as sending out anyone to cover him. It's not the best situation, although if anyone can deal with it, it's Kade."

"It makes sense to get the sheriff and police chief involved. What I don't understand is how Heath and the others can do anything against an attack by a gang."

"You should've been here in the fall. Kade extended his leave to recuperate from an accident and talked Heath into working with everyone on their shooting and self-defense skills. Even the women had to learn. He called it a mini-boot camp," she snorted. "It wasn't mini as far as I could tell. Unless traveling for business, everyone attended all day every Saturday for a month, plus he worked with individuals at night. And this was long before he'd heard about the threat."

"It's good he's taking the danger seriously." Amber thought of her own pathetic attempts to learn to shoot. She'd never taken a self-defense class, deciding a canister of mace in her purse would serve the purpose. Now she wondered.

"Guess who's next on the training schedule?" Brooke's mouthed curved into a smile.

"Me? Oh, no. Besides, I don't live at the ranch and I'm not part of the family. There'd be no reason to come after me."

"Kade already talked to Heath and Jace. Since you're friends with the Sinclairs, and will most likely spend some of your free time with us, they believe you should be prepared—just in case. Don't feel too bad about it. Mitch had to go through the same training when he came to Fire Mountain. You start this Saturday."

"This Saturday?" Amber groaned out the question. "I'd planned to look at bikes this weekend."

"Perfect. You can talk to Kade about where to look and who to talk to while he's training you. Trust me. It'll be fun."

******

"How's your schedule on Saturday? You have time for a ride?" Eric nursed a beer, keeping an eye on the new waitress at The Tavern, a locals hangout and sports bar.

"Can't. I'm working with Amber."

Eric's head snapped away from the waitress toward Kade. "Working with her how?"

"Shooting, self-defense. The same stuff I put you through last fall. She is a looker."

"Who? Amber?" Eric asked, narrowing his eyes on Kade as his body stilled.

"Well, yes, she's outright gorgeous. I'm talking about the waitress you've been eyeing since you came in," Kade snorted.

"Uh...yeah, she's pretty. So, why would Amber need training?"

"Heath and Jace believe since she's a friend of you Sinclairs, she needs to be prepared. No big deal. A few Saturdays. Brooke plans to join us when she can. You might want to stop by, get a refresher."

They both knew Kade's comment was in jest. Eric learned to shoot at a young age, progressing from shotguns, to rifles, and handguns. He, Cam, and their father had taken a couple of hunting trips each year until Kit Sinclair passed away. Eric always bagged his limit. He still went to the range each month, practicing and keeping his skills at a top level. Kade had once told him his talents were wasted in searching for real estate when he could be a deadly force hunting bad guys. Eric had laughed at the suggestion.

Eric stared at the half-empty glass of beer, losing the desire to finish it. He pushed it away and threw some dollars on the bar. "Can't. I have plans."

"Well, when you get finished with your *plans*, feel free to stop by and check her progress. At some point you might want to take over, help with her shooting skills."

"Not likely." Eric slapped Kade on the back.

Kade watched him leave, noting how he'd forgotten all about the waitress he'd been so focused on a few minutes before.

Chapter Five

Appleton, Texas

"He's gone, Robbie." Swinger hated giving his Prez bad news.

"What do you mean, gone? DEA agents just don't disappear." Robbie Morgan stood, pushing away the half-dressed woman who'd been sitting on his lap. "Get out," he snarled, motioning toward the door. She stumbled away, grabbing her blouse, not bothering to slip it on before slamming the door behind her.

"Explain." Robbie reached down to pick up his vest, revealing club colors tattooed on his back. He punched his tattoo covered arms through the openings, not bothering with the t-shirt crumbled at his feet.

Kade Taylor had once ridden with them, become a full patch member of Satan's Brethren, been a confidante of Robbie's, and had the respect of the leadership. He'd been welcomed as a fellow brother and one percenter, signifying his status as a member of an outlaw motorcycle club. Kade and Robbie had spent many nights drinking until they couldn't stand while club whores knelt before them.

He'd been one tough S.O.B., doing everything they'd asked, and never once giving a hint of his true affiliation. Turned out he worked for the DEA. Special Agent Taylor now had a target painted on his back, and the Brethren would be the ones to claim the kill before disposing the body in a place where no one would ever find it. No body, no crime.

"You called us back to Texas for other business right after he gave his deposition in San Diego. Now the boys can't find him." Swinger planted his feet, arms crossed, watching with narrowed eyes. "Hell, we didn't get the word from Sonny to go after him until a couple weeks ago. He could be anywhere."

Swinger had become the national enforcer after Robbie's father, the founder of Satan's Brethren, Sonny Morgan, was arrested, along with his top lieutenant and three other officers. It had been a miracle Robbie wasn't with them. Instead, he'd been meeting with a Satan's Brethren support club, setting up a hit on a rival gang encroaching on their territories.

His father had gotten word out he'd step down, letting his son take his place to take out the DEA agent who'd put him in jail—Kade Taylor. Robbie had been tapped to do what was needed to carry out the orders.

He'd sent several brothers to San Diego to confirm Taylor's location before finalizing his plans. He wanted all details nailed down tight before riding west with Swinger. Over the objection of each of his officers, he'd made it clear he'd be the one to carry out the hit—personally.

The news of Taylor's disappearance created a major problem. Even though Robbie held the national president position, his father still pulled considerable weight and more than a few people owed him favors. Several doubted the younger Morgan had the balls to the fill the position and build alliances, but didn't fight Sonny's decision. Robbie knew he had to prove them wrong.

He let out a loud curse before grabbing a cold beer and downing half of it. He needed this win to earn the trust of the chapters.

Swinger grabbed his own beer and paced toward the opposite wall, glancing out the dirt-encrusted window. "I can have the brothers follow Taylor's partner, Clive Nelson, and his buddy, Salgado."

"The U.S. Marshal?"

"That's the one. We've got four boys in San Diego, plus we can pull from the local chapter. It wouldn't take long to see if he shows up, or *persuade* the agent and the marshal to provide his whereabouts."

"Hell, Swinger, why don't you just send up a fuckin' flare, let everyone know we're looking for the guy? Roughing up his brothers will serve no purpose except to bring more heat down on us. We need to locate him without anyone knowing about it." Robbie took a long swallow of beer.

Although he didn't like it, Swinger nodded. "I'll pull our boys and have the local chapter watch the marshal and agent. Hands off—just follow them and report to me what they find."

Robbie nodded in agreement. "As I recall, he had a good hookup in Arizona. Some woman he'd been protectin'. Send the boys there, have them snoop around, see if they can find out if he's still connected with the broad. We can't wait until we know if Sonny and the others will go to trial."

"It may take some time." Swinger tossed his empty can in the trash.

"The trial could be months away. Find him and figure out what needs to be done. I want to know everything before riding out. You'll need to arrange an accident, something that can never be tied back to us. But, Swinger, I will be the one to finish this.”

“Understood.” Swinger grabbed the door handle. “And what do you want me to do about the other issue?”

“My daughter?”

Swinger nodded.

“Nothing.”

“Nothing?”

Robbie had waited twenty years to start a search for the daughter he gave up on Sonny’s command. He’d never risked his father’s wrath trying to locate her before, not even taking the chance of contacting his friend, Crystal, in Wyoming. Now that Sonny sat in jail, and most likely would be on his way to prison within the year, Robbie wanted to find her. It would have to wait a little longer.

“We’ll find her, just not yet. We have more important matters to deal with, such as DEA agent, Taylor.”

“Right.” Swinger turned to leave.

“And Swinger.”

“Yeah.”

“Send the whore back in.”

✱✱✱✱✱✱

61

"Widen your stance a little. That's right. Now aim and squeeze the trigger." Kade stood behind Amber as she held the Glock 9mm.

Although she'd spent much of her life on her parent's ranch in Colorado, she knew the basics of using a firearm and not much more. Her early years included learning to ride and care for horses, eventually leading to some amateur barrel racing, the same as Heath's daughter, Cassie MacLaren. Amber's parents had sold their ranch her first year in high school, deciding to move to California to be closer to relatives. That's when she'd met Eric.

"I missed," she groaned and looked over her shoulder at Kade.

"By a hair. Try it again. We have plenty of time."

She went through the motions again, this time piercing the outside ring of the target.

"I got it!"

"You did. Now do it again until it's empty."

Amber finished and released the magazine as the sound of an approaching motorcycle drew her attention. She shielded her eyes from the bright sun, watching as the rider brought the bike to a stop near the ranch house. He removed his helmet, shook his head, and turned toward her. Eric.

He hung the helmet on the handle bars, crossed his arms, and leaned against the bike, never letting his gaze leave hers.

"Will he bother you?" Kade asked, not wanting Amber to lose her concentration.

"Of course not. What's next?"

"Load the magazine and do it again. Three more times, then we'll break for lunch. Afterwards, you'll use a rifle."

Forcing herself to concentrate, Amber went through the rounds, improving each time. Even though her arms ached, she felt a huge sense of satisfaction when they broke for lunch.

"Great job." Kade clasped her on the shoulder.

He retrieved the target while Amber picked up the extra ammunition. They walked to the house as Annie came out and stood by Eric.

"I thought I heard you ride up. You'll stay for lunch, of course."

"I don't think—"

"Have you eaten?"

"No, Mom, I haven't eaten."

"Good, because I have plenty. How'd she do?" Annie asked as Kade and Amber walked up.

"I can definitely hit the side of a barn," Amber joked.

"You can do a lot better than that. Look here." He held up the targets showing her improvement with each round.

"Looks good, Amber. Now, all of you, come on inside. I'm sure you're starving."

Eric followed them in, wondering why he'd decided to stop by. Mitch had other plans, so he decided to go alone. He'd ridden for two hours before taking the turn toward the house. He could've gone another route to his place and avoided seeing Amber work with Kade. Instead, curiosity won out. Now he'd be forced to spend more time around her, being cordial. He'd done enough of that at work all week.

No matter his resolve to never let her get close to him again, he couldn't stop his body's automatic reaction to her. After all these years, she remained the one woman who could heat his blood with a glance. Seeing her each day at work was torture. He'd taken to working out an extra half hour in the company gym to get his body back on track. Then she'd walk by or be in the same room and he wanted to take another cold shower. After just one week, his frustration had hit a boiling point. He knew it would never work for them again, not ever. Too much baggage and bad memories. If only his body would accept it.

"When's your next trip?" Annie asked Eric, who sat beside her.

"I fly out Wednesday for Austin. Hope to be back sometime Friday." The mention of Austin brought an image of Jax to his mind. Perhaps he'd call her, see if she wanted to spend time together Thursday night. She may be just what he needed to purge Amber from his thoughts—at least for a while. As time passed and he adjusted to her being around, he had no doubt his reactions to her would change and she'd be just another colleague.

"Doesn't Brooke fly out to Cold Creek next week?" Annie looked at Kade.

"Monday. They'll review the findings from her visits before the honeymoon, plot out what needs to be done. It's good timing, as Jace has me traveling next week."

They'd just finished when Brooke came racing in. "Sorry I'm late." She looked at her husband. "We have a slight problem."

"Which is?" Kade asked.

"I forgot we committed to a ride with Lainey and Cam this afternoon. They're outside saddling the horses." She shrugged, giving him an apologetic look.

"Guess we'll pick up again tomorrow, if that works for you?" Kade asked Amber.

"It's no problem."

"Why don't you go with us? We won't be out long, maybe a couple of hours and you'll be able to get back on a horse." Brooke looked to Kade for confirmation.

"Well...I—" Amber started.

"Great idea. I'll go get another horse ready." Kade got up and headed out the door, not waiting for the women to hash it out.

"Why don't you come too, Eric? It's a beautiful day and who knows when the weather will change." Brooke shot an expectant look at her brother, hoping he'd agree.

"Can't today." He stood and carried his empty plate to the counter, then glanced at his watch. "In fact, I'd better get going. I've got a hot date." He leaned down and kissed his mom's cheek then headed toward his bike without another word, leaving the women to stare after him.

Amber watched him leave, feeling an emptiness she hadn't expected. Of course he'd have a date, and a hot one. She doubted he ever spent a night alone—him with just the television for company. He'd never been one to pass up a good time, and she doubted he had any concept of being lonely.

She thought of her parents and how they'd struggled since their accident a few years before. Amber doubted Eric had any idea of what had happened. He and her dad used to have the best times playing tennis, golfing, and trying to outdo each other on the BBQ. They'd been as upset with her as Eric when she left for New York. Of course, they'd forgiven her. He never would.

"Hey, Amber." Brooke waved her hand in front of Amber's face. "You with us?"

"Oh...yes. Let's go." She took the hat and gloves Annie held out and followed Brooke to the barn. A few hours of riding would do her good, and as the horses came into view, she began to feel the same excitement as always when she had the opportunity to ride. Perhaps she'd get a motorcycle and a horse as soon as she saved enough money.

******

He'd worn a heavy sweater, leather jacket, gloves, and face guard. Still the cold wind bit into his skin and chilled his body. Eric needed it. The brisk air, fast bike, and miles of road. He'd lied about having a date, needing to put some distance between him and Amber. She seemed to have accepted his presence with such ease, feeling none of the affects he did when they were together.

The fact being near him didn't seem to bother her at all ate at Eric. It had been the same when she'd left him standing in the driveway the day they'd packed her car for the drive to New York. She'd never once looked back.

What the hell was wrong with him that he couldn't accept she'd never loved him—at least not enough to stick around? There'd be no reason for her to have issues dealing with him now when he meant so little to her years ago. The truth about their relationship had never been easy for him to accept. As much as he'd hoped she'd come back, try to regain what had been thrown away, she never did. A couple emails a year and nothing more. She'd been sentenced to a spot reserved for those he'd purged from his life. It was a spot she shared with no others.

It hadn't been a deliberate lie when he told Cam and Kade he no longer loved her. He'd been telling himself the falsehood for so long, he'd come to believe it himself.

Eric turned into a shopping center flanked by a gas station on one end and a convenience store on the other. In between stood a liquor store, nail salon, Mexican restaurant, and a bar whose main clientele consisted of locals—people who had nowhere to go on a Saturday afternoon. Perfect.

Almost all spots were taken. He slipped in between a couple of trucks and turned off the engine. Inside, all tables were full, leaving one seat at the bar. He grabbed it, ordered a beer, and looked up at the three TV screens mounted above the bar. One basketball game and two replays of older football games. Not much, but better than heading to his place and watching TV solo.

He sat back and nursed his beer, thinking of Amber and how best to deal with his conflicting emotions. There had to be a way to sever reality—knowing they'd never be a couple—and his body's instantaneous reaction to her.

Eric tilted the beer to his lips, hearing the various conversations around him. From behind him and to his right, he heard someone mention the name *Taylor*. He swiveled in the direction of the conversation, this time hearing another male voice say *MacLaren*. In a corner sat three men, a fourth standing in front of them. None were familiar.

Eric twisted toward the bar while pulling his phone from his jacket and disabling the flash. Using his jacket to partially hide it, he pointed the phone toward the corner and took three shots, thankful the noise level in the bar drowned out the clicking sound. He slipped it back in his jacket as strong fingers gripped his shoulder and spun him to his left. Attached to the hand he saw a medium height man with a protruding belly and dark beard sprinkled with gray.

"What you got there?" The menace in his voice accompanied a stoney stare.

"Something bothering you, friend?" Eric asked, noting another man walking up behind the first. He saw nothing to indicate biker affiliations and recognized neither.

"Yeah. I want to know what you have there in your pocket."

"No offense, but that would be none of your business." Eric moved to turn back when strong hands slammed him into the bar.

"Hand it over."

"What's going on here?"

Eric recognized the voice of Buck Towers, the Fire Mountain Police Chief. He turned toward him, noting the civilian clothes.

"Hey, Buck. Good to see you."

"Sinclair. Anything going on here I can help you with?" Buck eyed the men. At well over six feet and over two-hundred-thirty pounds, few people messed with Towers.

"It's none of your business, mister. I'd suggest you stay out of it."

"Well, you see, I don't believe I can do that." Buck produced his badge, watching as the man's eyes widened. "You care to tell me what's going on?"

The man backed away, holding his hands out, palms up. "It's nothing. Just thought I knew this man."

"Guess you don't," Buck said.

"Guess not." He turned and walked back toward his friends.

Buck took the empty stool next to Eric, still keeping watch on the three as he ordered a beer. "What was that about?"

"No idea. Guess he just took a dislike to me. Never saw him before."

"Do you recognize the others?"

"Nope. Glad you showed up. I wasn't looking forward to taking him and his friends on by myself."

"I almost didn't stop. My wife is in the valley, visiting friends, so nothing to rush home to." He took a sip of his beer, then glanced around the bar once more. "I heard about the suspected threat against Kade. You know anything more about it?"

"Wish I did. He spoke with the agent assigned to take his place, and all he knows is Kade's name is circulating among the biker community."

"Which is never good."

"Not much we can do without specifics. We're as prepared as we can get. You haven't noticed any outside biker activity have you?" Eric asked.

Buck shook his head. "Kade would be the first to know if we spotted anyone suspicious."

"Any chance you recognize the men at the table to your right?"

Buck looked over at the three men seated at the corner table. "They're all locals. All three work construction. Why?"

Eric glanced at the table to see the fourth man they'd been speaking with had vanished.

"Probably nothing. I thought I heard them mention Kade's name." Eric finished his beer and set the empty glass on the bar. "Guess I'll head out."

"I'll walk out with you. I don't like what I saw happening and want to be sure you're not followed."

Chapter Six

Eric pulled into the ranch as Kade and the others rode across the north pasture toward the barn. He'd forgotten how good Amber looked on a horse—fluid, as if she and the animal were one.

"Hey, Eric. You staying for supper?" Lainey asked as she slid off her horse. "Annie invited all of us after you took off."

"I believe I will." Eric had made the decision while nursing his beer to approach his discomfort with Amber as he would anything else—head on—forcing himself to spend time around her. After a while, she'd become just one more member of the management team and not the woman he'd once loved.

"Kade, do you have a minute?" Eric walked up beside him.

"Sure. What's up?"

Eric nodded toward the house. "I have something you should see." They walked into Heath's office and closed the door behind them. Eric pulled out his phone. "Look at this."

Kade studied the picture. "Where'd you take this?"

"At the bar near the crossing. Do you recognize any of them?"

"The one seated with his back to the wall. As I recall, I met him at the same bar a couple of times last summer. He works construction. The other two I don't recognize and the fourth has his face turned away. Why?"

Eric explained what he heard and what happened with the other man and Buck after he took the picture. "It may be nothing."

"Doubtful. What usually happens is three or four will go inside a bar, restaurant, wherever there are people who may have the information they need. One will split off to ask questions, leaving the others to keep watch. Were the others wearing colors?"

"Neither Buck or I saw anything to associate them with a gang, although they wore leathers. You might have been able to recognize their bikes, but I had no idea what to look for."

"Send this to me and I'll forward it to J.D. Montalban. He's the agent who they brought in to replace me. I've known him for years and trust him implicitly. He's also a good friend of Nesto."

Kade and Ernesto "Nesto" Salgado had known each other since before high school, working as wranglers on a ranch in Montana until they'd both enlisted in the Army, moving into Special Ops together. Nesto had gone into the U.S. Marshal Service after the Army, while Kade had accepted a position with the DEA. Nesto and Brooke's close friend, Paige Wallace, had become an item when they met on the ranch the previous summer.

"I've got to tell you I sure don't like the idea someone's after you. Seems to me the DEA should send men out, give you the protection you deserve. After all, you are the key witness." He slipped out of his heavy leather coat and slung it over his shoulder. "We'd better join the others before they come looking for us."

******

"How did you have time to fix all this between the time we left and now?" Amber's stomach growled as she looked over a spread including chicken enchiladas, carne asada, tamales, Caesar salad, rice, black beans, various salsas, and chips.

"I've learned to be prepared. You have to when most of your family lives within a few miles of you." Annie's pride in her and Heath's blended family never wavered.

"I don't know where to start." Amber grabbed a plate.

"Follow me and take what I do. You won't go wrong."

Eric's warm, silky voice came from behind her, sending unwanted shivers through her body. She shook them off and glanced over her shoulder at him.

"Sounds good." She let him walk past her, took the same items in smaller amounts, and still ended up with a plate filled to overflowing.

"Sit by me. We can talk about some ideas I have for the Austin property." Eric indicated two places on one side of the long table.

"All right." Amber's brows furrowed in confusion. He'd barely tolerated her all week, been rude more than once, and now he acted like none of it had ever happened. Her senses on alert, she took her seat, pushing it a few inches away, creating whatever space she could at the crowded table.

"Sorry I'm late." Heath walked in, tossing his hat on a nearby table and kissing Annie on the cheek. He filled his plate and sat next to Annie, at the same end of the table as Eric and Amber. "How'd your lessons with Kade go?"

"Great. I can't believe how much I improved within just a couple of hours. He's a great teacher." Amber had decided to frame the last target and put it in her apartment.

"She didn't get through as much as I'd hoped. Something came up," Kade added from further down the table. "We'll work on self-defense tomorrow, and if there's time, we'll do more target practice."

"I may join you for that." Eric tipped up his bottle of water and took a big gulp.

"That so?" Kade asked.

"You said I could use a refresher, so..."

"Tomorrow morning. Seven o'clock in the family room." Kade referred to the huge room at the back of the ranch house with thick carpet.

Amber and Eric groaned at the early hour.

"How about nine?" Eric asked.

"Or even eight?" Amber added.

"Wimps. Okay, I'll compromise. Eight, but no later." Kade rested an arm around Brooke's shoulders. "And wear comfortable clothes."

******

Amber fell into bed, tired from a day of practicing with the 9mm and riding. She renewed her love of horses and vowed to ride with Brooke as often as possible. It had been one of her best days in a long time, also one of the most confusing.

Eric had progressed from being cold and aloof to joking and conversing as if they were still close friends, at one point resting a hand on her shoulder before snatching it back. It had been heartbreaking how the camaraderie had mimicked their life together years before. Her body had buzzed from the mental, emotional, and physical contact they'd shared until she had to distance herself from him, no longer able to handle the conflicting emotions.

She rested the crook of her arm over her eyes, blocking out the light from the moonlight seeping through the curtains. What was she to do now? Her heart pounded hard throughout dinner and afterwards as they'd taken seats in the family room, at Heath's suggestion, to watch a movie. There hadn't been a good time to excuse herself without appearing rude. If Heath wasn't her boss, she may have felt more comfortable making her exit right after dinner.

Eric had taken a seat on the same deep, comfortable sofa where she'd settled, resting a leg against hers several times during the movie. She didn't understand how he could be so oblivious to the electricity surging through her each time his muscled thigh brushed hers. Worse, her breath had caught when he removed his heavy sweater after dinner, revealing a tight fitting black t-shirt that accentuated his taut chest. He'd filled out since college. His shoulders had broadened and his biceps were evidence of a committed exercise routine. She'd had to turn her back to him to keep from staring. Even now, laying alone in her bed, she felt her body respond and squirmed to get into a more comfortable position.

From what Brooke told her, he hadn't been shy about dating over the years, and she wondered what he'd learned from his various lovers. By contrast, her encounters had been few and unsatisfying. She swallowed the lump in her throat and closed her eyes tight, wanting to erase the images of Eric with other women. Her musings could do nothing except cause more confusion. He no longer saw her as a desirable woman who caused his blood to boil, and she'd learned the hard way he wasn't the man for her. If she ever did meet the right man, he'd at least be able to talk through their differences—a concept foreign to Eric.

She threw off the covers and padded to the kitchen, filling a cup with water. Perhaps tea would calm her enough to sleep.

Eric woke early from a restless sleep. He'd drifted off sometime around two after trying to read, then watched TV—nothing calmed the intense desire he felt for Amber. He'd been so certain his actions the night before would lead to a lessening of his attraction toward her. It had been the opposite.

It was a mistake to sit next to her at dinner and during the movie. Her unique scent, the sound of her voice, and feel of her leg against his had triggered all the same sensations he'd felt years before when they'd been a couple. He grabbed his phone, knowing Kade would already be up and working through his daily exercise routine. Forcing himself to train with her today would be foolish.

"Hey, Eric."

"I didn't wake you did I?"

"Not likely," Kade snorted. "What's up?"

"I'm not going to make the training this morning. I'll have to do a refresher after I return from Austin."

Kade's silence told Eric his brother-in-law's interrogator mind had gone on alert—not a good sign.

"I get it, bro. You need to keep your distance from Amber. No problem. We'll set something up on a separate day and time when you return."

"Hey, I never said it had to do with Amber."

"You didn't have to."

Eric sat on his bed and took a breath. "I realized last night that it's better to keep my distance. Too much history and no future. It makes no sense to voluntarily be around her more than what I already have to in the office."

"I get it, man. Don't worry. I'll tell her something came up. If I don't see you, have a good trip to Austin." Kade hung up as he walked into his bedroom to see a still sleeping Brooke. His heart swelled at the sight of her. He couldn't imagine losing her, then being forced to be around her as Eric had to do with Amber. Life could be a real beast.

******

Austin, Texas

"Welcome back, Eric." Keith Vance extended his hand then indicated a chair. "Have a seat and I'll grab us coffee, then we'll go over the details of your offer."

Eric relaxed in the comfortable leather chair in Keith's office and looked around, noticing the incredible view to his left. The wall behind the desk held credentials, university degrees, and certifications. A large bookcase spanned the entire wall to Eric's right. He glanced behind him to see a large wooden file cabinet, the entire wall above it covered in pictures of what appeared to be family and friends. He stood and walked over to it, bending closer when he spotted a picture of Keith and two women—one was Jax Perry.

"I understand you and Jax had a chance to get acquainted." Keith held two cups of coffee and kicked the door closed as he approached Eric.

"We did." The last person Eric wanted to speak with Keith about was Jax. He'd considered calling her, arranging to see her while in Austin, but he'd never made the call.

"She's a talented marketing person. Her company has grown by double digits since she came back to Austin, focusing on development and construction clients. You might want to consider her for MacLaren projects." Keith picked up the offer Eric had emailed him a few days before and glanced over it.

"I have no doubt her ideas would prove to be quite inventive. However, we've just hired a Director of Marketing. She'll be handling marketing for all of our groups." Eric assumed he'd been introduced to Jax for the purpose of learning more about her work. He estimated they'd discussed her professional work for perhaps five minutes of the ten hours they'd spent together.

"At some point all companies need an infusion of new ideas. You might want to keep her in mind. Well, shall we start?"

Eric drove back to his hotel, confident their offer would be accepted with few negotiations. They'd offered the seller a fair price and terms, plus Keith had an excellent relationship with the other broker. He expected to hear back from Keith the following morning, leaving him with a free night and wondering how to fill his time.

He pulled out his phone, found Jax's number, then hovered over the call button. They'd had a great time before and both were single. Whatever happened would stay between them. He had nothing to worry about. Then why didn't he push the button?

Eric scrubbed a hand over his face and scanned the view of downtown Austin through the large picture window. By all accounts, it was a happening city with popular clubs along Sixth Street and restaurants and bars on South Congress. Any other city, at any other time, he'd jump at the chance to check out the nightlife. It didn't take much for him to know what had changed. Amber.

He'd avoided her all week, missing the weekly management meeting to take a conference call with Jace and Rafe, then leaving for Austin. His plane would take off Friday at two, in time for him to land in Fire Mountain for a date he'd scheduled weeks before with a woman he'd gone out with several times. She'd moved to San Francisco months before, coming back every six weeks to visit her family, and him. Their arrangement had always been casual. She'd stay at his place a night then fly home. No entanglements. Funny how she no longer held any appeal to him.

Eric picked up the phone and dialed. Room service and a movie would have to do.

Chapter Seven

Appleton, Texas

"You were right. He's in Fire Mountain. Seems he left the DEA and works on a ranch owned by some wealthy locals—the MacLarens. And get this, he married the woman he'd been protecting." Swinger tossed a cigarette to the dirt and ground it under his boot.

They stood under a large tree several yards from the old house used as their headquarters on the outskirts of town. The land and buildings had been purchased years before and sat in the middle of forty acres. They'd built an underground bunker, complete with separate rooms with bunks, a kitchen, and bathrooms. Years before, Robbie designed a secure room where weapons and extra ammunition were kept. Few people knew the access codes to the double door entry and Swinger made certain the codes were changed on a regular basis.

The location in the middle of nowhere assured them of spotting anyone who approached uninvited. Unmarked graves at the outermost section of the property testified to the club's commitment to keeping their affairs out of public view.

Swinger looked to the ground, noting the hundreds of cigarette butts littering the area around the tree, a testament to the years it had been used as the unofficial spot for private discussions. He glanced up, letting his gaze roam the area. Although few of the brothers or club whores were outside, Swinger shook his head at anyone who ventured too close.

"Married." Robbie thought this over, his mouth twisting in a wry grin. Men with old ladies were more vulnerable than those with no ties. "Where's he living?"

"Some place on the ranch. Don't know specifics, but I'll find out."

"Do I have to tell you he can't find out we've located him? We don't want the DEA to send agents out like the last time."

"How were we supposed to know the woman was connected to some drug cartel and they'd sent extra agents to help? We lost brothers in that mess," Swinger spat out, his expression feral. Another reason he and Robbie wanted Kade in the ground.

"Forget it. Find out where he lives on the ranch and get back to me. And start tracking his old lady. I want to know everything he does, if he travels, who his friends are, if he has a whore on the side—everything." Anger welled inside Robbie, fists clenching at his sides as he remembered the way the club had been worked by the shithead they'd called brother. The betrayal would not go unpunished and that included anyone close to Kade. They'd take them all out to get to him—women included.

"Hey, Robbie!"

Joker, one of Robbie's bodyguards, motioned to them.

He nodded toward the man then turned back to Swinger. "I want you to handle this personally. We can't afford any fuck-ups."

"Whatever you want, Robbie. When do you want me to leave?"

"Tomorrow. And take Joker with you."

"Who'll protect you if both of us leave?" Swinger and Joker were Robbie's primary protection from anyone who wanted to get to him. Anyone who knew Robbie understood the two men would lay down their lives protecting him and killing whoever got in their way.

Robbie crossed his arms and glared at Swinger. "You don't think I can take care of myself while you're gone?"

"Look, Robbie—"

Robbie dropped his arms and slapped Swinger on the back. "I want my two best men, plus the ones you already have in Fire Mountain on this. Nothing can go wrong." He turned toward the house then looked back over his shoulder at Swinger. "I expect you and Joker to be on the road at first light tomorrow."

******

Fire Mountain

"What did you think?" Annie asked Amber as they both left the MacLaren Foundation monthly board meeting. She'd been invited as a non-voting member to observe and offer suggestions. Heath and Jace planned to get her involved in their foster care community outreach, the main focus of the foundation's efforts.

"It's impressive. Everyone's prepared and the programs are much better than what I'd expected."

Annie glanced at Amber, her mouth tilting up. "You mean for being an out of the way town?"

"I don't mean it as a slight. It's just I've been involved in different foster care support groups in big cities, and they aren't half as together as you are. How long have you been on the board?"

"Heath brought me on not long after Jace's wife, Caroline, recommended me. She and I have been friends for years, and she knew I had a passion for helping foster care children."

"Were you and Heath already dating?"

"Not at all. He was enjoying his single status too much and dating women several years younger to notice me. Kit had been gone a couple of years and I wasn't looking for a relationship. We did become good friends, though. About a year later we discovered how much we wanted to be with each other." Annie shrugged. There was quite a bit more to it, but that would be a story for another time.

"I was sorry to hear about Mr. Sinclair."

"You were at his service but didn't come to the reception."

Amber's eyes widened at the comment. "You saw me?"

"Eric pointed you out. I think he was disappointed you didn't come up afterwards."

"It's complicated, Mrs. MacLaren."

"Please, call me Annie. I'm sure it was as complicated then as it is now." Annie saw something pass across Amber's face. Regret, perhaps? Or maybe resignation that the past couldn't be reclaimed. "Well, you have a good start here. Heath is quite impressed with you, and that's saying a lot."

"I've been here just two weeks."

"Oh, I think you'll find he's a pretty good judge. It's not often people fool him." Annie glanced at her watch. "I'd better get going. It was good to see you and I'm thrilled you're taking an active role in the organization."

Amber sat in her car, thinking back to Kit Sinclair's funeral. She hadn't thought any of them had noticed her. She'd stayed near the back, not wanting to interfere. He'd passed not long after she'd left for New York and she still felt raw at the sight of Eric. Kit and all three of his children had been close, but Eric had a special bond with him. He'd looked so lost that day, sitting between Annie and Brooke. Cam sat on the other side of their mother, holding her hand and looking as desolate as the others.

Within a year of Kit's death, her own parents had their accident, changing their lives and the lives of Amber and her two brothers. Even with their ongoing medical needs, her parents insisted their three children continue on with their lives and not worry about them.

Her stomach growled and she realized how late it had gotten. She could head to the store or grab dinner out. Her stomach rumbled once more, making the decision easy. Brooke had told her about a family restaurant favored by locals.

She figured it would be crowded on a Friday night, and it was. She put in her name and waited until a booth near the back became available. The waitress brought her a glass of wine and took her meal order when she heard a familiar laugh, causing her stomach to tighten and her breath to hitch.

Amber shifted enough to see the hostess showing a pretty young woman to a table across the room. The hostess set down another menu and turned to leave when Eric walked up, taking a chair next to the woman, his back to Amber. She stared a moment longer, a lump forming in her throat, then looked away. At least he hadn't seen her. She'd eat her dinner and leave before he had any idea of her presence.

******

"Hello, Eric, Marion. I haven't seen either of you in a while." A man about Eric's age came up and shook his hand.

"Marion just got in this afternoon, so we thought of your place."

"Glad you did. What can I get you?"

They ordered then Eric sat back and picked up his drink, taking a sip before broaching the subject he'd tried to address on their way to the restaurant.

"I—"

"You should've seen the chaos at the airport. The weather was horrible and there must have been at least ten planes circling to land." Marion took a hearty swallow of her red wine. "Then they had to escort someone off the plane. I didn't hear what happened, but I could hear the man complaining all the way out the door."

He'd forgotten how Marion loved to talk. Cute and feisty, she could be entertaining or frustrating, depending on his mood. Tonight he fidgeted, having a hard time keeping his mind on the conversation. When their meal arrived, Eric dove in, letting her continue talking until she'd wound down and picked up her fork. He let her eat a few minutes, enjoying the silence, then decided he had to let her know his change of plans.

"We won't be going to my place tonight."

Her brows shot up at his words and she set her fork down. "Oh? What's come up?"

"Nothing's come up. I guess some things have changed with me, and, well..." he didn't know how to continue.

She sat back and crossed her arms. "Sounds like you may be over us."

He took a breath and leaned forward. "I think that may be the case."

"I see." She offered a weak smile that didn't reach her eyes. "It's all right. We've had good times and there's never been any expectations." She scrunched her eyes as if thinking. "Have you met someone?"

"Perhaps. It's amounted to nothing so far."

"But you'd like there to be something?"

He took another sip of his drink, swirling the ice in the glass. "Yes, I would."

She reached over and placed a hand on his arm before leaning over to kiss his cheek.

"Then I hope it works out for you. You deserve someone special." This time her smile did reach her eyes and Eric felt a sense of relief.

He'd made a decision. Now he'd have to see if it would go anywhere.

******

Amber watched the interplay, feeling as if she were snooping on his private life. Uncomfortable, she ate a few more bites, paid, and walked outside, hoping Eric didn't spot her. He deserved his privacy and she needed to get far away from him and his date.

She almost made the turn to go toward her apartment when she spotted a café specializing in coffees. The latte she'd planned on after dinner evaporated with the turn of events at the restaurant. She'd passed by this small, intimate coffee house a few times, never having the time to stop. Inside were large, comfortable lounge chairs, small tables for two, dim lighting, soft music, and a mix of couples and singles. The latte came up within minutes. Picking it up, she saw the one spot left was a table with two chairs and grabbed it.

Amber took a sip, then grasped the cup with both hands, needing the warmth to counter the chill she'd felt at the cool night air. She pulled her phone from her purse and scrolled through emails and texts, answering some, ignoring others. Dana sent a text with an image of her new apartment, then a selfie with her standing in the kitchen, holding a glass of wine and smiling.

"Excuse me. There don't seem to be any seats left. May I join you?"

She looked up to see a nice looking man standing across the table from her, his hand on the extra chair.

"Be my guest."

He took a seat, setting down his cup, and shirking out of his coat. "This is a great spot, but there are never enough chairs."

"This is my first time coming in and I had to hurry to grab this after a couple left."

"I'm Dylan Newcastle." He reached his hand across the table.

"Amber Anderson. Nice to meet you." She sent a quick text to Dana then slipped the phone into her purse.

"I'm guessing you haven't lived here long if you haven't been here before."

"A few weeks. I moved from Denver to accept a new job. What about you?"

"I came here almost a year ago. Moved from the valley to join my uncle in his orthopedic practice." Dylan glanced over the rim of his cup. He guessed Amber to be a few years younger than him and one of the prettiest women he'd seen in a long time.

"What do you think of Fire Mountain?" Amber asked.

"It's a wonderful town, good people, and lots to do, especially if you like being outside." Dylan sat back and stretched his legs out. "So where did you accept a job?"

"MacLaren Enterprises. I'm doing their marketing, or at least trying to get my arms around their different companies," she joked.

"I've met Mrs. MacLaren a few times, as well as her husband and sons."

"Oh?" Amber should've known. Seems everyone knew the MacLarens, and by extension, the Sinclairs.

"Through my uncle, Dr. Barry Newcastle. Are you settling in all right?"

"So far. I work a lot so haven't had much time to get to know the area. I'd love to find a group that hikes." She finished her latte, ready to leave and yet wanting to learn more about Dylan. "I guess it's time I head home."

"Would you mind if I called you sometime? I do some hiking and perhaps we could meet when we both have a free day."

"I'd like that. Here's my card." She scribbled her personal phone number on the back. "I'm free most weekends unless I'm traveling. It was nice to meet you, Dylan."

"Likewise, Amber. I'll look forward to seeing you again."

She drove home feeling much better than when she'd left the restaurant. Dana had been harping at her for months to get out, like tonight, where she might have a chance of meeting other single people. Perhaps Doctor Newcastle would call. A sense of anticipation washed over her at the prospect, something she hadn't experienced in a long time. Maybe Fire Mountain would turn out to be the place where her life finally came together.

Chapter Eight

"One more time." Kade watched as Amber made a forceful, upward motion with her hand, palm up. "That's it. Now do the series of moves we practiced today."

She learned fast, making it possible for him to cover more exercises than planned. They stopped for lunch then reviewed what she'd learned in the morning. Kade glanced up at the clock on the mantel.

"Do you have time for some target practice?"

"Definitely. I'll get my coat." She dashed toward the entry, feeling energized, then stopped when Brooke walked in, covered in snow. "It's snowing?"

"Started on my way over here. It's almost a blizzard out there now." She slipped out of her coat.

"Well, darn."

"Why?"

"Kade and I were headed out for target practice. Guess it'll have to wait until tomorrow."

"Or the storm could pass by, then clear up. We'll wait it out." Kade walked up to Brooke and wrapped an arm around her before pulling her close for a kiss. "Hey."

"Hey, yourself." Brooke looked up at him. "I wouldn't count on it clearing."

"Might as well wait half an hour. If it doesn't improve, we'll call it a day. Sound good?" He looked at Amber.

"Works for me."

"Where's Mom and Heath?" Brooke walked toward the kitchen, opened the refrigerator and pulled out a soda.

"They didn't say where they were going." Kade grabbed a water and one for Amber.

"Hmmm. She asked me to stop by after lunch. Wonder what she wanted?"

"Whatever it was came up kind of sudden from what I could tell. She took a call, then found Heath. They left a few minutes later." He picked up an apple and bit into it as the front door opened and Annie walked in, Heath right behind her. Heath barely glanced at them as he shrugged out of his jacket, then leaned down to kiss Annie.

"I'll be in the office." Heath didn't say another word as he closed the door behind him.

"Is he all right?" Brooke asked her mother, whose somber look worried her.

"Let me get something to drink and we'll talk." She grabbed a soda and took a seat at the table.

"What is it, Mom?" Brooke kept her voice low, not wanting to pry, even though she knew something wasn't right.

"Jace called right after lunch. He and Caroline were at the hospital with Blake. He hasn't been feeling well, so the doctor put him through a battery of tests. They just got the results."

"And?"

"He's been diagnosed with testicular cancer."

"Oh my God." Brooke put a hand to her mouth and turned toward Kade, who'd been talking with Amber.

He sat down, putting his arm around Brooke. "What's going on?"

Annie explained what she knew then fell silent. "It's in the early stages, so there's every reason to believe he'll beat it. It's just a lot for a young man to handle." She pushed from the table. "I'd better see if Heath is all right. He didn't want to leave the hospital, but Jace insisted."

Amber stood near the front windows, not sure what to do, but knowing something awful had happened. Brooke motioned her over and she took a seat across from them at the table.

Brooke looked up at her with moist eyes. "Jace and Caroline's oldest son, Blake, has been diagnosed with cancer. That's why they left, to meet them at the hospital." She laid her head on Kade's shoulder. "He's only twenty-two."

Amber hadn't met Blake. She'd heard of him and his younger brother, Brett, and knew both attended college in Texas.

They heard the door to the study open. Heath and Annie walked out and grabbed coats before joining the others.

"I've spoken with Trey and Rafe. I couldn't reach Eric, Cassie, Cam, or Mitch." Heath looked at Brooke and Kade. "Would you make sure they know?"

"Yes." Brooke reached over and grabbed Kade's hand.

"We're going over to Jace and Caroline's. They've brought Blake home and want to discuss the available options with us. I'm not certain when we'll be home." Heath noticed Amber for the first time. "We don't generally share much about family personal matters. I'd appreciate it if you didn't say anything at work. Blake worked in the offices last summer and most everyone knows him."

"Of course, Heath. Anything they learn should come from one of the family."

Heath put an arm around Annie. "We'd better go."

Kade followed them to the door. "What else can we do?"

"There isn't anything right now. I'm not certain how long we'll be gone, but you're all welcome to stay as long as you like."

Kade closed the door behind them and pulled out his phone. "Hey, Mitch. I have some news you should know about."

******

"Here's what I've found," Lainey said, walking in with a stack of papers. "The information discusses all the stages, from symptoms to the various treatment options."

Brooke and Kade had been able to contact the rest of the family. Everyone, except Cassie, congregated in the great room, talking and trying to understand what might happen with Blake.

102

"And survival rates?" Eric asked. He and Blake had become close over the summer when Blake worked in his department.

"Yes. I've made several sets." Lainey passed them out.

Amber stayed in the kitchen, fixing coffee and setting out food, which drew little interest. The ranch house kitchen, eating area, and living room had been designed as a great room, making it possible for a large number of people to congregate and not feel cramped. Normally full of laughter and loud voices, today the room had fallen into an eerie silence as everyone read the material Lainey gave them.

Cam read the information, then tossed down the papers, and sat back on the leather sofa. "If it is in the early stages, it appears Blake has a lot of choices and a good chance of a full recovery."

"I saw him driving his truck earlier in the week and wondered what he was doing here in the middle of classes." Eric picked up his cup and headed into the kitchen for more coffee. He hadn't said more than a couple of words to Amber, who now leaned against a counter, her hands clasped in front of her.

She looked at the deep furrows in his brow as she filled his cup and handed it to him. "I should go."

Eric reached out and grabbed her hand. "Stay. Please."

His eyes had a similar look as the day of his father's funeral. She didn't want to intrude, yet couldn't refuse if that's what he wanted.

"If you're sure. I don't want to be in the way."

"You won't be." He squeezed her hand

The door flew open as Cassie dashed in, tossing her coat and gloves aside before rushing up to Brooke. "Any news?"

"Heath and Mom haven't returned from Jace's. Lainey found quite a bit of information on what Blake has." She offered Cassie the material in her hand. "Here, read this while I get you some coffee."

Cassie settled onto the sofa to read, glancing up at Cam or Eric several times as she began to understand her cousin's illness. "Do we know if it's stage one?"

"It is, which gives him a good chance of recovery." Cam sat next to her, putting an arm around her shoulders. "Trey and Jesse know what's going on. We'll keep them posted."

Cassie's older brother, Trey and his wife, Jesse, both Naval Aviators, were stationed in California. Their jobs and young son, Trevor, made it hard for them to get to Fire Mountain as often as they'd like.

They all turned at the sound of the front door opening. Annie and Heath hung up their coats before joining everyone in the great room. A sea of expectant faces stared at them as they took seats.

"He's scheduled for surgery tomorrow morning." Heath scrubbed a hand over his face as he leaned forward. "The doctors believe his chances are good if the cancer has remained localized."

"Lainey found a lot of information about the surgery. Do they know yet if he'll get an implant?" Brooke asked, knowing the topic wasn't pleasant for any of them.

"Blake's opted to have the implant during the removal surgery, unless the surgeon finds a reason not to go ahead with it. He's done a lot of research in the last twenty-four hours and is taking it all pretty well. The doctor told Jace and Caroline he'd be in the hospital a couple of days, then they'll put him on an x-ray and testing schedule, which will last for years to make sure nothing has spread." Heath stood and paced to the bar, pouring glasses of scotch for him and Annie. "I think Jace is more upset than Blake. Plus, they're battling Brett who wants to fly home. They've told him to stay at school. They're hopeful Blake will return to Texas within a couple of weeks."

"He's always been strong—physically and emotionally." Cassie stepped next to her father and wrapped her arms around him. "I'm still worried about it, though."

"We're all worried, sweetheart. Nothing is guaranteed and even though he's in excellent physical condition, his recovery could take longer than they anticipate. There's also the chance the cancer has spread beyond what the initial tests show."

"What time is the surgery?" Eric sat next to his mother, taking her hand in his.

"Seven-thirty. I'm driving Blake and Jace to the hospital, and Annie is taking Caroline."

"How big is the waiting room?" Mitch asked.

"Big. Anyone who wants to wait there is welcome. Annie and I are going to grab something to eat then head to bed. Whoever is out last—"

"Lock the doors," Cassie said, glancing up at her father and offering a vague smile.

"We're going to head out. We'll see you at the hospital tomorrow." Cam grabbed Lainey's hand.

"Same with us." Brooke and Kade gave Annie a hug before following Cam outside.

Within minutes the house cleared out, except for Eric and Amber, who stood together at the kitchen island, talking in quiet voices while Heath and Annie prepared plates with food Amber had set out.

"We're heading upstairs," Annie said as she followed Heath out of the room.

Without a word, Amber began to wrap and store the remaining food, saying nothing to Eric who helped clean up. She placed plates and glasses in the dishwasher then wiped down the counter.

"I'd better take off." Amber picked up her purse and jacket.

"I'll walk out with you."

"Please let me know how it goes tomorrow," Amber said as she pulled the key from her purse and slid into the car. She tried to start the car three times, but the engine wouldn't turn over.

"It may be the battery. Pop the hood and I'll attach cables between your car and my truck." Eric pulled the truck close to hers and attached the cables. They tried several times, not getting any reaction from Amber's car. "Seems like your battery is gone. We can check it out tomorrow after Blake's surgery."

"I can call my road service and they'll come out tonight. Don't worry about me. You can go ahead and take off."

"Forget it. I'll take you home tonight and you can call the road service in the morning. Come on." He leaned over and pushed opened the passenger door.

"I should leave a note for your parents—"

"I'll let them know."

She climbed into the cab and closed the door, already regretting the confinement of the small space. The truck smelled of a mixture of leather, aftershave, and Eric's unique scent—a combination which triggered a reaction so powerful she found herself inching toward the door, trying to get as far away as possible.

"I don't bite, you know." He smiled, a rueful, crooked upward tilt of his lips.

She glanced at him, ignoring the warmth creeping up her face. "Of course you don't bite."

He chuckled at her indignant tone before shifting his gaze to the front and accelerating.

The short drive seemed to take hours as Amber worked to ignore her discomfort. Something about riding in his truck, at night, with him sitting so close, brought back memories she wanted to bury. He'd owned a similar truck while in high school and college.

They'd spent many nights making out until they'd finally succumbed to what they both wanted and spent the night together in a hotel near campus. They'd been freshmen in college and she knew, without hesitation, he was the one man she'd want for the rest of her life. Sitting next to him, years later, the painful truth latched onto her. He was still the one man she wanted and the one man she couldn't have.

"You'll need to give me directions." Eric shot a look at her as he pulled to a stop at a red light.

"Up three blocks then turn right. It's in the middle of the block on the right."

He pulled to a stop, opened his door, and walked around to her side.

"I can get it," she said, stepping on the running board then to the ground.

"I know." He turned to face the building and saw the entry gate. "Nice complex."

"Phyllis put me in touch with someone who'd heard of an opening. I was lucky to get it." She slung her purse over her shoulder and looked up at him. "Thanks for bringing me home. I'll take care of the car tomorrow."

He ignored her comment and cupped her elbow with his hand. "I'll see you to your door."

"That's silly. I come home alone every night."

"True, but tonight you'll get an escort."

They walked through the gate and up the stairs to her place, her heart racing as she tried to put the key in the lock. Her hand shook so much she had to take a shallow breath to calm herself. The key slid from her hand, dropping to the ground.

"I'll get it." Eric bent down and picked it up, sliding the key into the lock and releasing the deadbolt. He pushed the door open and let her step inside, his eyes darkening as they locked with hers.

She couldn't look away. Being here with him wasn't right—not for either of them. They'd made their decisions years ago, found new lives, and left the other behind. Then why couldn't she break the hold of his gaze and look away?

Chapter Nine

The trip to her apartment had been excruciating. Not so much because of where she sat, within arm's reach of him. It had more to do with his acceptance he still loved Amber, wanted her back in his life and his bed—always. No other woman had been able to find a way into his heart the way she had, and there'd been many who'd tried.

He'd spent the drive trying to come up with the right words, something to make her understand he'd never stopped loving her. The fear she'd turn from him again began to fade as the need to find out if they could ever have a future took over. He'd seen the way she watched him when she thought he wasn't looking. The regret he'd seen almost choked him.

It had taken all his willpower to unlock her door and step aside instead of taking her in his arms. Now he found his control falter as she stared up at him.

His chest squeezed as his breath caught. He reached for her hand, turning it over to press his mouth to her palm, never taking his gaze from hers. Her lips parted, her breathing quickened. The air around them pulsed as if they'd been enveloped in a magnetic force neither could escape.

"Amber..." He whispered her name a moment before lowering his head until his mouth came down on hers. The first touch seemed almost tentative before he wrapped his arms around her and tightened his hold. The kiss deepened, his mouth devouring hers, hot and moist.

He could feel her hands move up his arms to wrap around his neck, pulling him tight, melding her body to his. He groaned as her tongue traced his lips, sending a hot ache through him. Gathering her closer, he explored the recesses of her mouth until he pulled away on a ragged breath, letting his lips trace a path down her neck to the soft spot at the base. He sucked lightly before moving back up to reclaim her mouth.

Amber's caution shattered at the first touch of his lips to hers. It had been so long and she wanted him so much. The feel of his mouth devouring hers sent waves of heat pulsing through her. She remembered how they used to be together and began to feel the same sense of urgency. Her hands moved under his jacket, splaying across his back.

"Ah, baby," he groaned as fire roared through him. "God, I want you."

Even though her mind had fogged, caution raced through her. She didn't want to let go, break the spell, yet the fear of starting anything with him stalled her motions. She pulled away, burying her head in his chest, and loosening her grip on his back.

"Eric," she breathed out. "What are we doing?"

Amber hated the way his body stilled. At the same time, warning signals urged her to slow down. She'd wanted this since seeing him on her first day at MacLaren, had dreamed of it, waking in a heated sweat, twisted within her sheets. But she needed to know why, after all this time, he wanted her.

Eric hadn't felt her lips against his in so long. He missed the urgent heat and total loss of control her touch had always caused, yet her question stopped him. He pulled back, resting his forehead against hers, breathing heavily, his mind clouded from the feel of her against him. He stepped away, brushing bangs away from her eyes, then letting his fingers trace a line to her chin.

"I'm sorry. This shouldn't have happened—not like this."

She wrestled with the extreme disappointment at his words. What had she expected? A declaration he still loved her, needed her, and wanted her back in his life? She wasn't a child. He'd received difficult news and needed the closeness she provided—nothing more. The chemistry between them had always been strong. Too many times they'd resolved disagreements by falling into bed, letting sex fix whatever stood between them.

He saw the same regret he felt reflected in her face and wished he could stay, knowing it wouldn't be right. "Don't misunderstand me. I want you so damn much it hurts, but not like this, not without clearing up our past." He breathed in a ragged breath as he dragged a hand through his hair.

She stepped away, trying to calm her still shaking body.

"You're right. This was a mistake." She paced a few feet away, turning her back to him, and taking a deep breath. She crossed her arms and turned toward him, not believing there was any chance of *clearing up their past*, as he'd phrased it. "We made our choices years ago. We'd be kidding ourselves if we thought it could ever work again."

Eric stared at her, not accepting her words. "I didn't say it was a mistake. It's just..." his voice trailed off as he fought for the right way to say he still loved her. He walked the few feet to the sofa and lowered himself into it, leaning forward, drawing his knees up and resting his arms on them before burying his head in his hands.

Amber sat next to him, resting a hand on his thigh. "What is it?"

He dropped his hands and shifted toward her, settling his hand over hers.

"Don't you know?"

Her senses went on alert. Was he trying to tell her he'd found someone and had fallen in love? Maybe it was the woman she saw him with in the restaurant. She leaned away, trying to prepare herself for whatever it was he wanted her to know.

"Hell, Amber. What I'm trying to say is I love you. I've always loved you. Never stopped."

"Eric—"

"Please. Hear me out. I thought you were in my past, gone from my life for good. Then you showed up here, forced me to face the fact I'd never gotten you out of my system. It's just..."

In her heart, Amber thought she knew what he wanted to say. She didn't want to hear it, yet knew it was the truth. "We've caused each other too much pain to be together again."

"Perhaps. And that's the problem. I don't know if we can put it all behind us and make it work." He turned her hand over and rubbed circles on her wrist with his thumb, feeling her jolt at the sensations.

He didn't believe it would be difficult to get her into bed, take what he wanted, and walk out the door. They'd learned years ago how to ignore the real issues between them and let their lovemaking soothe their differences. They were too old to play those games any longer. Besides, he couldn't do that to either of them.

Amber could see the remorse on his face. It spoke to her more clearly than any words. He wanted her, said he still loved her, but he might never trust her again. And if she were honest, she had no desire to be with a man who would cut her off as Eric had done before. He'd given her an ultimatum without giving her a chance to explain. She'd made up her mind long ago not to be controlled by stipulations or settle for anything less than a full partnership, something she doubted Eric could offer.

She pulled her hand from his and pushed away, creating some distance.

"It nearly killed me when you gave me a choice to stay or go without hearing the explanation of why I wanted to try New York. You never even considered my request, just dismissed it and told me I had to choose. I tried several times to get you to talk about it, but you refused. You were so calm and controlled when we packed my car, never once indicating any regret, just acceptance. It took a long time before I realized you'd never loved me as I'd thought. If you had, you'd never have let me drive away. Leaving you was the worst thing I've ever done."

He didn't want to hear how his actions may have caused the split, or if he'd handled it in a different way, she might have stayed. In his mind, all the blame rested with Amber and none with him. Had he been fooling himself all these years?

"I admit I've never thought about it from your side. Then again, I never believed you ever considered how moving to New York would affect me and my plans."

"That's because you refused to discuss it." She rubbed her eyes with the palms of her hands, trying to relieve the tension and clear her head.

Eric saw her exhaustion and knew nothing good would come of a discussion unless they were both prepared for it. He'd pushed too hard, surprising her, and perhaps hurting his chances at a second chance.

"It's late and tomorrow will be a long day. We both need some sleep. I'd better leave." He stood and took the few steps to the door before turning back toward her. "I do love you, Amber. I did then and I do now. I don't know if trying again will work, but I'm willing to give it a shot if you are—whatever it takes, everything I have. But I won't bring it up again until you let me know you're ready. You need to decide for yourself if what we had is worth a second chance."

He pulled the door closed behind him, leaving Amber alone and conflicted. She sat frozen in place, unable to move as she processed his last words. The sound of his footsteps faded into the distance, yet she still couldn't rise from the sofa. Her hands were clasped so tight the knuckles had turned white. She took a shaky breath and stood.

From her front window she could see Eric get into the truck and pull away. Part of her wanted to run after him, say she'd do whatever it took to try again. Another part warned her it could be a fool's journey to another broken heart. She'd grown comfortable in a life filled with work and her close friendship with Dana. Her new job couldn't be better—challenging and surrounded by people she respected, which included Eric. The decisions to buy a horse and a motorcycle were hers alone. She needed no one to approve or disagree with what she wanted to do. She had an independent life and saw no reason to change it—until now.

******

The family crowded into the private surgery waiting room, some standing, others seated, waiting for news of Blake. Jace paced back and forth, had since they'd wheeled Blake away. Caroline was a rock, keeping him together since they'd first gotten the diagnosis.

All heads turned as the doctor came through the door, walking toward Jace and Caroline.

"He's in recovery and everything looks good. As suspected, the cancer was localized and we believe we got all of it."

"Thank God." Jace pulled Caroline into his arms and kissed the top of her head. "And a prosthesis?" he asked.

"Done. He'd already consented and we saw no reason to wait." He looked around the room, noting the number of people. "He'll be able to see two people at a time, but for tonight, just Jace, Caroline, and maybe a couple of others. Blake should be feeling good enough to see anyone who wants to visit tomorrow."

"Thanks for everything." Jace extended his hand before Caroline gave the doctor a hug.

"I'll be around to check on him later today and again tomorrow. I'm glad it turned out the way it did." The doctor left, leaving the family to rejoice over the good news.

"Why don't you and Caroline stay? The rest of us will stop by tomorrow." Heath clasped his brother on the shoulder. "If you want, I'll call Brett, tell him all is good."

"Thanks, but we'll call him, then he can speak with Blake when he's coherent." Jace offered a tired smile full of relief. He'd slept little and gotten up at four-thirty to get Blake to the hospital.

"Tell Blake we're all thinking about him and to prepare for a roomful of family tomorrow."

"Will do." Jace turned toward Caroline, then swiveled back to Heath. "And thanks. Having everyone here meant a lot."

******

Eric left the hospital feeling a huge sense of relief at the success of Blake's operation. He pulled into the MacLaren lot, spotted Amber's car, and parked several spaces away. He would do what he promised—not pressure her and give her space. She'd need to come to him if she wanted to try again. In the meantime, he had a full schedule to keep up with and potential new properties to assess.

"Eric, Keith Vance is on the phone for you. Do you want me to take a message?" Phyllis asked as he walked past her desk toward his office.

"No, I'll take it." He hung up his jacket and grabbed the phone. "Hello, Keith."

"Good afternoon, Eric. Hope I'm not interrupting anything."

"Not at all. What can I do for you?"

"You mentioned wanting to expand your holdings in Austin, and I've just picked up the listing on a set of properties which might interest you. The owner has properties in Houston, also.”

“It never hurts to look. When will you have all the details together?” Eric asked.

“It’ll take a week or more. I’ll let you know. It might be an opportunity for me to come out to your place, make a presentation on the properties as well as the other services we discussed.”

“That might work. Keep me posted and I’ll see what can be set up.” Eric made a note to speak with Heath and Jace about Keith’s call.

“I’ll be in touch.”

Eric had been impressed with Keith and his company. Having him travel to Fire Mountain to meet the rest of the management group might prove fruitful in securing other deals. The added benefit would be Keith meeting Amber. Once they met and he saw some of her work, he’d understand why Jax’s company wasn’t an option.

The rest of the day passed without incident. He packed up at seven, noting Amber’s car was already missing from the lot. He hadn’t seen her at all, which given their recent encounter was probably for the best. Dinner and bed sounded real good. Tomorrow he’d go straight to the hospital.

******

"Sorry I couldn't take your call, Dana. I'm at home, so call me when you—"

"I'm here, Amber." Dana's breathless voice sounded as if she'd just run up a flight of stairs.

"Hey. I got your message earlier. Crazy day or I would've called back sooner. What's the emergency?"

"Not so much an emergency as the grapevine at work is running overtime. It's all hush-hush, but it sounds like the company is having significant financial problems and may have to lay off a bunch of people."

"How'd you hear about it?" The news didn't surprise Amber, she'd heard rumors for months of missed payments, quality issues, and a sales slump.

"At lunch with a friend from accounting."

"Ava?"

"You know I can't tell you that." Dana's incredulous tone told Amber she'd guessed right.

"Right. Okay, so what did Ava say?" Amber asked, getting a laugh out of Dana.

"She's been preparing numbers each week on certain trends and they aren't improving. In fact, they're tanking. They called her at home over the weekend, asked her to come in and run department numbers by employee with their salaries. She worked with someone from human resources for a couple of hours. That's all I know. What do you think?"

Amber held the glass of wine she'd poured before calling Dana and leaned against the kitchen counter, listening to Dana's news. Even though distressing, it pulled her mind from Eric and their conversation the night before.

"Doesn't sound good. It wouldn't hurt to start looking for something else, unless you want to find out if they offer some type of severance package."

"So you think Ava's right to be concerned? She came on board about the same time I did, is single and has two kids. "

"I don't know if she's overreacting or not. I doubt she'd mention it at all if she didn't have a pretty strong sense a layoff was being considered." Amber had been reviewing expenses for outside services at MacLaren. One of the biggest was graphic design, Dana's field. "Look, let me do some checking where I work. Maybe they'd have some interest in bringing the design business inside."

"That'd be great. I'll start looking for possibilities here. As you know, anyone associated with the marketing group tends to be first to get the boot."

"It's always been like that. I'll let you know what I find out."

"Anything happening with Eric?"

"Nope. Not a thing." She felt bad lying to Dana, but wasn't prepared to share what she and Eric had discussed, at least not yet. She needed time and a clear head. "I haven't eaten and am starving. I'll call you later this week. Keep me posted if you hear anything else."

"I will. Goodnight."

"Goodnight."

Amber set down the phone and poured a bowl of cereal, having no desire to cook. She'd seen Eric's truck when she left work, feeling a slight clenching of her stomach at the reminder of their talk. It had been on her mind all day. In truth, she hadn't been able to rid her thoughts of everything that happened with him yesterday. It had been so long and he'd felt so right. If she hadn't broken the spell, asked the question, they may have ended up in bed, waking up together this morning with nothing resolved.

Amber finished her cereal, then opened and closed cupboards, inspecting her supplies. She'd already heard from Cassie about the success of Blake's operation. It didn't seem right for her to stop by the hospital when she hadn't met the young man. Instead she decided to bake and put it all in a basket for someone to deliver to his room. At least she'd feel as if she were doing something for him without intruding on the family's personal space.

She went to work, and by midnight inspected a beautiful array of her mother's favorite recipes. Food she'd made for Amber's brothers, Ryan and Jake. She packaged and set it next to the front door before changing and climbing into bed. Perhaps tonight she'd be able to fall asleep without dealing with the continual images of Eric or remembering the feel of his lips on hers.

Chapter Ten

"Delivery," Rafe called as he walked through the door to Blake's room, carrying a large basket filled with assorted cookies and brownies. He set it down and handed the card to Blake, nodding at the others in the room. He'd just flown in from Montana, wanting to see Blake and also visit with his sons, Mitch and Kade.

Blake opened the envelope and read the card, smiling as he closed it up.

"Well, who's it from?" Jace asked.

"Someone named Amber Anderson." He shrugged, unfamiliar with the name.

"Well, that was sweet of her." Annie reached for the card and read it. "As I recall, that girl can bake."

"You know her?" Blake asked.

"We all do. She's the new Director of Marketing," Heath said.

Blake's eyes widened at the news and he shot a look at Eric. "This wouldn't be *the* Amber, would it?"

Eric shifted from one foot to another, crossing his arms across his chest. "I don't know what you're talking about."

"Come on, Eric. The Amber who was the model in the magazine ad you had on your desk last summer. I saw it during one of our meetings. Knock-out figure, stunning smile, unbelievable—"

"Fine. I remember, and yes, it's the same woman."

Blake's self-satisfied smile irritated Eric, but he shrugged it off.

"Did you see her in the hospital?" Blake asked Rafe.

"She was downstairs handing it off to a nurse to bring up when I saw her. I offered to take it."

"Why didn't she just come up herself?" Annie asked.

"Don't know. She was talking to a Doctor Newcastle. Followed him into the cafeteria as I left." Rafe took off his hat and set it on a nearby table, glancing at Kade but saying nothing.

"The older Dr. Newcastle or younger one?" Annie asked.

"How should I know?" Rafe asked. "About Cam and Kade's age."

"Ah, Dylan Newcastle, the hunk," Cassie interjected, remembering the doctor from when Annie had gone through her physical therapy.

"Hunk? I wouldn't call him a hunk." Eric shifted again, clearly unhappy with the direction of the conversation.

"You're not a woman. Trust me. The man's a total stud. I wonder how Amber would know him." Cassie's brows knit together. "I sure wish he'd notice me."

Lainey laughed. "Cassie, you may not realize it, but you have guys falling over you all the time. You're just too busy to notice."

"Excuse me. I need to grab some coffee." Eric strode out of the room, never breaking stride as he took the elevator down and walked toward the cafeteria.

"What was that about?" Heath asked as he glanced at Annie.

"I haven't the foggiest," Annie replied, although she thought she might have an idea.

******

Eric grabbed a cup of coffee and searched the room, finding Amber sitting at a table with Dylan Newcastle. He'd met the doctor when his mother had gone in for her follow-up visits with his uncle, Barry Newcastle. From what he could tell, both were excellent doctors and both were single.

He made his way through the tables until he stood beside Dylan and extended his hand.

"Dylan."

He looked up, and recognizing Eric, stood to shake his hand. "Eric. It's good to see you again. Please join us. Amber mentioned Blake MacLaren is in the hospital. Hope it all goes well."

Eric took a seat, nodding at Amber. "According to his doctors the surgery went well. He's in great spirits, although still in pain. They hope to release him tomorrow or the following day." He glanced at Amber. "Rafe brought up the basket. You should go to Blake's room and let him thank you in person."

"I hope he likes everything. They're the recipes mother used when she sent food to Ryan and Jake when they were in college."

"All I know is he was tearing the wrapping open when I left. Apparently hospital food isn't substantial enough for a six-foot-four football player. How are your brothers?"

"Good. Busy with their jobs, some of which they can't talk about." She looked at Dylan. "Both my brothers are younger than me. Ryan graduated from the Naval Academy and Jake from West Point."

"I'd like to meet them sometime." Dylan took a big swallow of his soda, wondering at the relationship between Eric and Amber. They seemed to know each other pretty well for her brief length of time in Fire Mountain.

"The truth is I'd like to see them, too," Amber joked. "I can't recall the last time we were all together for Christmas, or any holiday. It's all right, though. They're doing what they love and both are happy."

"Guess I'd better get back to my rounds. Eric, it was good to see you again. Give my best to your family." He glanced at Amber. "I'll look forward to seeing you on Saturday." Dylan pushed from the table and walked out.

Amber focused on Dylan's empty chair, avoiding Eric's gaze. She didn't want to explain anything regarding Dylan and wasn't prepared to talk about the two of them. Not yet.

"Are you dating him?" Eric's voice had turned flat and cold.

"Not that it's your business, but no, we aren't dating. He knows I haven't been here long and asked if I would be interested in hiking with him and some friends on Saturday. I said I would."

Eric's jaw worked, but he didn't respond. He'd opened himself up the other night, hoping they might have a chance. He didn't know what to think of Dylan's obvious interest in Amber or her desire to spend time with him. Maybe friendship, maybe more. He sure as hell didn't like it.

"I see. Well, I guess I'd better go back upstairs. Consider stopping by and introducing yourself to Blake. He'd like to meet you." He stood and turned toward the door.

"Eric."

He looked over his shoulder at her.

"About Dylan—"

"You were right. It's none of my business."

Amber gripped her empty cup, a knot forming in the pit of her stomach as she watched him disappear through the doorway. She'd been surprised and pleased at Dylan's invitation. It hadn't occurred to her to say no. Dylan had offered it as a way to meet more people, get to know the town and what went on. There'd been no indication he saw it as anything more, and neither did Amber. Eric obviously had.

She had to find time to talk with him, try to find a way to sort through their past and decide if trying again was truly an option for them. She sighed, knowing she now faced a bigger hurdle than even an hour before.

******

Eric didn't go back to Blake's room, deciding space and fresh air would do him more good than a closed room filled with family. Besides, his current mood didn't lend itself to casual banter. What he wanted to do was slam his fist into a wall. Instead, he side-stepped a patient in a wheelchair and strode through the automatic doors to the parking lot. The cold, brisk air peppered with snowflakes slammed into him, stinging Eric's face.

He muttered a curse as he continued toward his truck. His desk remained piled high with folders of past, current, and proposed projects. A new intern would be arriving in the afternoon, ready and eager to begin her three month assignment in marketing. The following week he had a busy travel schedule. There'd be little time to focus on Amber and her interest in Dr. Newcastle. At least that's what he told himself as he pulled into traffic. He'd push her out of his mind and concentrate on what he could influence, not what lay well outside his control.

Appleton, Texas

"Give me some good news." Robbie took the steps two at a time into the house and slammed the door shut, letting one of the new prospects stand guard. Both Swinger and Joker had refused to leave until they'd identified three brothers to take their place watching out for him.

"Followed him from the ranch this morning. He had a woman with him who fits the description of his old lady. They drove to the hospital and haven't come out yet. Been two hours." Swinger sat on his bike, turning his back to the cold wind. "He's getting sloppy. Didn't appear to be checking for anyone at all."

"Stupid bastard probably believes he's safe," Robbie smirked.

"Good for us. Too damn bad for him and whoever he's with when we grab him." Swinger shifted on his bike, looking around and spotting a lone cop car a block away.

"Keep watching him and see if there's a pattern. Follow his old lady and any other women who come and go. We're gonna take our time and do this right. No more screw ups."

"Hold on." Swinger turned toward the entry door to see Kade and several others walk out together. They stood in a circle, talking for several minutes before getting into their own cars. "He just walked out with several others. I don't recognize any except Taylor and his old lady, but I'll find out who they are."

"Locate his place, see if we can grab him there."

"That may be hard. He lives on the ranch, and there's only one way in and out from what I've seen. The road takes you within spitting distance of the main house. It would be almost impossible to get in and out without being seen." Swinger turned away as Kade drove past him. Neither he nor Joker wore their colors and doubted the ex-DEA agent would connect them with Satan's Brethren. For all Kade knew, they were just two citizens out for a ride.

"Rent a car and drive in. If you're stopped, tell them you're lost but go as far as you can. I want to know every possible way to get to the son of a bitch or his old lady before making a decision on how to get rid of him. The man's vulnerable."

"The rest are pulling out and headed in the same direction. I'll get back to you." Swinger slid the phone into his jacket and took off with Joker right behind. They stayed a good distance back, heading out of town toward the ranch. At the entrance, a couple of cars pulled in while others continued straight. Kade stayed on the road. The two bikers didn't turn, Swinger deciding to find out where Taylor would lead them.

All the cars pulled into a complex of office buildings a few miles from the ranch entrance. Swinger and Joker pulled to the side of the road and stopped, waiting until everyone had parked and gone inside before riding to the front of the building. He looked up at the name on top. *MacLaren Enterprises*, the same name as the ranch where Taylor worked.

They rode to the house they'd rented on the outside of town, parking next to several other bikes. The owner insisted on a six-month lease for the several acre property with a large house, garage, and a couple of sheds.

"What's the word?" one of the other brothers asked as Swinger and Joker pushed open the door. They stripped off their citizen jackets, replacing them with their Satan's Brethren cuts.

"Got a good look at Taylor and his old lady. We spoke with Robbie. Joker and I'll be renting a car tomorrow, making like we're citizens, and try to find his house." He looked at Joker.

"Something nondescript, like one of those silver four-door boxes you see everywhere."

Joker just grunted. He hated riding in a car, didn't even own one, the same as most of the brothers.

"What do you want us to do? It's fuckin' boring sticking around in this old place." The same man paced to the window, pulling back a curtain and glancing outside. "At least let us pick up some hardbodies to take away the edge. The boys and I know where we can find a couple who'd be more than willing."

Swinger glared at his fellow brother. He'd been a prospect until a few months ago, young and ready for action. He was also a hothead, tending to make rash decisions. At the same time, they'd been cooped up a few days now with little to do.

"No girls from Fire Mountain. You want a couple whores, find them somewhere else, and make sure they get home. They don't see how to get here, got that? Party all you want tonight but not so the cops get wind of anything. Afterwards, we stay inside for as long as it takes. No drinking or partying until the fuckin' pig who'd betrayed Sonny is on his way to hell."

Chapter Eleven

"Yes, Phyllis?"

"The new intern is here to see you. Shall I send her back?"

"That would be fine. Thanks." Eric remembered meeting her once before Christmas, but didn't recall a lot about her. Between holidays, travel schedules, and her exams, the internship would be getting off to a later start than normal. It suited Eric fine. He'd give her the same load and see how she handled it. He opened his door as she came down the hall.

"Hello, Jillian. It's good to see you again."

"Mr. Sinclair. It's great to be here." She flashed an excited smile at him.

He let her pass by him, remembering the interview and her upbeat, friendly attitude. She'd worked her way through college as a waitress, preferring nights to a day job. Her references and grades were excellent, and if he recalled right, she'd grown up about forty miles away in a small ranching community.

"Have you been able to find a place to stay in Fire Mountain?" Eric grabbed his folder on Jillian and the one he'd prepared listing her intern duties.

"I thought I'd stay at home and commute each day. It's a little hard to rent a place for just three months and a motel room is too expensive." She fidgeted with the strap on her purse as she spoke.

"You live, what, thirty or forty miles from here?"

"Almost forty. But it's fine. There isn't much traffic."

"Tell you what, let me check to see if we might be able to come up with something a little closer that might suit you." He picked up the phone and dialed Phyllis. "What's the status with the employee apartments? Good. Put one aside for Jillian until June. Thanks."

"The company keeps a few apartments available for employees and interns. They're clean, furnished, and about fifteen minutes from here. You only pay utilities, no rent. What do you think?"

"That would be wonderful." She beamed at him.

"Good, then let's get to business. Afterwards, Phyllis will get you a key and give you directions." He slid the folder over to her and went through her assignments until a knock on the door interrupted them.

"Oh, sorry. I'll come back later."

"Wait, Amber. I'd like you to meet Jillian Walker. She's my new intern. Jillian, this is Amber Anderson, the Director of Marketing, the woman I told you about." He returned his gaze to Amber. "I have a heavy travel schedule for the next couple weeks, so Jillian will be working with you in my place. I've gone over her assignments and what she'll need to do. We've set up daily phone calls, and of course, I'll be available by email and conference call whenever you need me." He ignored the stunned look on Amber's face and continued. "In fact, now might be a good time for you to bring her up to speed on what you and I've been working on."

Her brows scrunched together before she recovered, plastering a smile on her face. "That would be fine. I wonder if I might have a few minutes with you before then."

He glanced at his watch. "I have a couple of meetings, then a dinner to attend. Would tomorrow morning work or is it critical to see me now?" He expected the chilled expression she sent him, then marveled out how fast she recovered.

"No, tomorrow is fine. I'll have Phyllis put me on your calendar. Why don't you come with me, Jillian? There's a lot going on and I don't want to hold Eric up." She shot him a pointed glare, knowing full well he was putting her off in his most gracious, condescending way.

She felt terrible about the way he'd left the hospital, thinking her and Dylan had something going. Eric had caught her off guard when he'd confessed to still loving her. It had been the last thing she expected, but then, she'd never expected him to kiss her senseless or her reaction to him after all these years. Her mind had gone blank, and looking back, she knew they would've ended up in bed if he hadn't made it clear anything more would be a mistake.

Then he'd opened up, crushing her understanding of their split. He might have cut her heart out that day, but now Amber realized, she'd done the same to him. Their selfish, immature responses may have cost them years of happiness, and now she hoped to find out if he meant what he said about second chances.

She'd stopped by his office to ask him if he'd consider having dinner with her, see if they could still find common ground and a starting point to rebuild what they'd lost.

Dr. Newcastle was a complication thrown in at the least opportune time. Besides being smart and a gentleman, Dylan Newcastle might well be the most physically gorgeous man she'd ever met. Amber hadn't realized what a good sense of humor he had until they'd had coffee at the hospital, and it surprised her how much she looked forward to the outing on Saturday. At least she had until Eric's reaction to seeing them together.

"Amber, wait up."

Jillian took a seat in Amber's office as Eric came down the hall. "I'll be right in, Jillian." Amber turned toward him, her arms crossed over her chest. "Yes?" She arched a brow. He couldn't be more wrong if he thought for a moment his pompous attitude would help get them back together.

He slowed his stride, stopping a foot away, and slid his hands in his pockets. The determined, unapologetic look in his eyes warned her he felt no remorse for his behavior.

"Do you have a minute?"

She almost said no, then changed her mind. "Mitch is in a meeting. We can talk in there."

They walked into the office next to hers, Eric closing the door and leaning against it.

"I wanted to thank you for taking on Jillian without warning. She's a good kid. Just needs direction. I think the two of you will hit it off and she'll learn a lot from you."

Amber waited for him to go on. When he didn't, she stepped toward the door. "Sure. If that's it, I'd better get started with her."

"Wait." He pushed from the door and strode to the window, looking through the blinds to the darkening skies, then turned back toward her. "Look, I know the other night came out of nowhere. I hadn't expected to say anything to you, at least not for a while, but it's out there and I won't take anything back. I realize you need time to decide if trying again is what you want. I already know my feelings, so it's up to you. From where I stand, you seem to need space, even though it sounds odd to suggest that after all these years."

"Eric..." her words trailed off when he lifted a hand.

"Maybe you do need to date, and Dylan Newcastle is a great guy. I wish he weren't." He swallowed the lump in his throat and took a deep breath. "I've thought a lot about what you said the other night, and you may be right. If I'd listened, asked more questions, maybe we'd be together today, married with kids."

He shrugged, then stepped closer. "The reality is, I didn't. So, I'll wait until you've made a decision. My schedule is stacked the next couple of weeks and I'm out of town more than in the office. You'll have plenty of time without me around to figure out what you want." Eric lifted her chin with a finger and gazed into eyes he wanted to see each morning and every night. "I'll accept whatever you decide. If you don't want to try again, there'll be no repercussions—at work or with family." His mouth curved into a slight yet sad smile that didn't reach his eyes. He dropped his hand and took a step back.

If she thought it was the right move, Amber would've launched herself into his arms, yet she held back. He'd given her what they both needed—time to make the right choice.

"You know we could decide to try again and it might not work out," Amber whispered.

"Are you afraid it won't?"

"Of course. Aren't you?"

This time he broke into an infectious grin which transformed his face. "Scared to death."

His smile and her nervous laugh broke the tension, and she reached out to take his hand.

"Thank you for giving me a reprieve. I've never been the most spontaneous person, and this..." she waved her hand between them. "I just need to think it through."

He pulled her hand to his lips and turned it over, placing a warm kiss on her wrist, then on the palm of her hand, sensing the shivers which rippled through her. "I want you, Amber. Think about that while making your decision." He turned and left, sucking all the air from the room as he closed the door.

Amber took a few minutes to compose herself. He'd offered her everything she'd dreamed of since she'd left for New York. She'd fooled herself for years trying to believe he meant nothing to her. The last few weeks proved her wrong. Her love for Eric had never died—not even close. Then why hadn't she simply told him yes, she wanted to try again?

Fear. An emotion she'd learned to live with many times over since moving east. Fear of failing in New York—which she had, and then was given a second chance by a producer who hated her acting and loved her ideas. Marketing had become her passion and she'd put her heart into it.

Life seemed good until her parent's accident and the gut-wrenching sense of being unable to handle all of their needs. With her brothers, Ryan and Jake, still attending college at the academies, the decisions had fallen to her until her father had awakened from his coma and recovered enough to take over. She could still feel the fear which gripped her each morning when she woke, knowing any day she might be called upon to make the decision no one should have to make.

She'd come through it to return to New York and a department layoff. The company she'd worked eighty-hour weeks to build, pulling all-nighters while caring for her parents, had brought in a national director who, in turn, brought in his own people. She left with fear the size of a basketball in her stomach and a fistful of glowing references.

It had taken nine agonizing weeks to land the job in Denver. She'd interviewed for openings in Chicago, Kansas City, Dallas, and Denver, and been offered positions in two of the cities on the same day, choosing Denver.

By that time she'd gone through a fifth of scotch and several bottles of wine while sitting around with her girlfriends on different nights in New York. They'd known of the gripping fear she tried to hide and would have none of it. Each had reached out to their contacts and helped her send out résumés, which led to interviews.

Throughout it all, when her fears overcame her common sense, she'd envision Eric lying next to her, his strong arms wrapped tight around her, whispering everything would be fine and he'd always be there for her, just as he had when they'd been together. Even though believing it seemed somewhat delusional, she drew comfort from the fantasy, and that comfort enabled her to move on.

Now he'd walked back into her life, tempting her with a second chance. Amber had to decide if she could find the courage to trust him a second time and take a chance on turning her fantasy into real life, or walk away, never knowing what might have been.

Chapter Twelve

"Pull." Eric saw the clay target fly through the air, moved the shotgun, and slapped the trigger, smashing the target into a hundred pieces.

"That's fifty straight—damn fine shooting. You want to go for an even hundred?" Kade asked. He, Mitch, and Eric had started their morning early at the rifle range before finishing at the skeet and trap range. All three had done well, with each besting the others at one point or another.

"Why not? I have nowhere else to go, and apparently, neither do you two." Eric grinned.

"I finally get back in town last night and Brooke picks today to go shopping in the valley with Cassie and Lainey. She was out of bed before me this morning. There's no justice." Kade followed the others to the first stand, preparing to start another round.

"Hell, man. At least you have someone to go home to. Eric and I have our TV dinners and beer." Mitch dumped a box of 12 gauge shells into his vest.

"Speak for yourself. I've upgraded to Italian takeout and fine wine." Eric glanced at the darkening sky then shot a look at Mitch.

"The hell you say. I bet you don't own a bottle of fine wine." Mitch's smug expression belied the resentment he sometimes felt toward Kade. He hadn't learned of the existence of his half-brother until a few months before. Of course, the news had been a shock to their father as well. Kade was the chronological winner by a few years, the offspring of Rafe and the woman he'd loved before meeting Mitch's mother. It had been a bitch to man-up and accept Kade, and some days were rougher than others, but at least he tried. His younger brothers were still working through it.

"I happen to know Eric does own fine wine because Brooke and I are the ones who gave it to him on his last birthday. She's working at bringing sophistication into our lives."

"Wine in gallon boxes doesn't count," Mitch countered, stepping up to the stand. "Pull."

They finished the last two rounds, Eric ending up with ninety-eight straight as opposed to the hundred he'd been after. He broke down the shotgun, placed it in its case, and locked the trunk.

"How about lunch?" Eric asked as the three climbed into his truck.

"You buying?" Mitch asked.

"Depends. You drinking?" Eric laughed, knowing Mitch's preference for more than one beer at lunch.

"I'll buy the drinks," Kade threw out.

"And I'll pick up lunch. I think it's my turn anyway." Eric pulled onto the highway, noting a group of bikers parked at a convenience store.

"Slow down," Kade ordered as he rolled down the window. "Citizens," he muttered before closing the window. He wasn't looking for recreational riders, those who made up ninety-nine percent of motorcycle owners. No, he searched for the one-percenters, the small fraction who belonged to outlaw motorcycle gangs, such as Satan's Brethren.

"You heard anything more?" Mitch asked. As much as he sometimes resented Kade, he didn't want any harm to come to him, or any of the family.

"Clive called yesterday, as did Ernesto. Both picked up tails and are certain they're being followed by members of the local Satan's Brethren chapter. Each has placed tails on the tails," he snorted. "Ought to be interesting." Clive Nelson was Kade's DEA partner before he left the agency.

"What do they think they're up to?" Eric parked at their favorite lunch spot and turned off the engine, shifting toward Kade.

"Since both are being followed, they think the club is trying to get a bead on me. Their guess is Robbie Morgan just realized I'm no longer DEA. Why the hell they followed them wearing their colors is anyone's guess. Pretty dumb move if you ask me." Kade shrugged. "And believe me, Robbie isn't anyone's fool. My sense is it's just a matter of time."

"Before they learn you're here?" Mitch asked.

"Right."

They remained silent as the waitress showed them to their table, their grim faces signaling the change in mood at Kade's news.

"What can we do?" Eric asked, taking a sip from his cup of hot coffee while glancing around the restaurant.

"Nothing more until we get some type of signal the Brethren are close. You two and the others are as prepared as you can be at this point." Kade smacked the table with his palm, drawing unwanted attention to them. "Shit," he muttered, picking up his cup. "The last thing I want is to bring a menace like Robbie and the Brethren to the family. If they do get this far, I plan to pack up and leave, draw their attention to me and away from you."

"The hell you will." Mitch's firm, low voice held its own level of danger. "There isn't a chance you're drawing anyone away from us. If they're after you, they're after all of us, and we take care of family."

Kade sobered at Mitch's words. Did he know how close his comment was to the mantra many motorcycle clubs used to rally their brothers? Probably not. Clubs saw themselves as a family. Except they were made up of those outside the normal boundaries of society.

He held Mitch's uncompromising gaze then clapped him on the shoulder. "I hear what you're saying and appreciate it. We'll take it a step at a time as we learn more." The comment needed to be said, although he still had no intention of putting any of his family in danger.

******

"How reliable is the information?" Heath spoke on the phone with DEA Special Agent J.D. Montalban as he walked away from the table

152

where he and Jace discussed further acquisition plans. "I see. I'll get in touch with him right away and have him call you. Yes, and thanks."

"More news?" Jace asked.

"A group from Satan's Brethren were spotted leaving San Diego a week ago, heading east on the freeway. The border crossing near Yuma confirmed several of them rode past. There weren't any confirmed sightings after that."

"And he's just now getting this to us?" Jace leaned back in his chair and crossed his arms.

"There was a massive communication screw-up between agencies. Agent Montalban just heard of it this morning. He's been trying to reach Kade for an hour. Do you know where he's working today, Jace?"

"He's taking the new client from Florida on a tour of our operations." Jace checked his watch, then glanced out the window. "It's almost noon. I expect him back here any time to meet me for lunch."

"If he's not back in thirty minutes, we go find him." Heath shot a glance at Jace.

"Agreed, but the Brethren could be going anywhere. Aren't they headquartered in Texas?"

"They are, but the odds are on the side of them heading north, toward us." Heath stood and paced across the room. "Kade knows them better than anyone. He'd be the one who'll have the most insight." Heath shook his head at the danger he believed was riding their way.

"What about notifying the others?" Jace stood and joined Heath at the window, which had an unobstructed view for miles.

"Eric and Mitch flew out this morning to inspect additional real estate deals. Cam's in Colorado with Lainey. As far as I know, Cassie and Brooke are in the office."

"And Amber?"

Heath turned toward Jace. "What about her?"

Jace crossed his arms. "We had her take instruction from Kade for this purpose. Besides, anyone would have to be blind not to see how she and Eric look at each other. My two cents? I think we need to include her as part of the extended family—at least for this situation."

Heath nodded then looked toward the street. "Here he comes now." He walked to his desk and grabbed the phone. "Phyllis, send Kade into my office as soon as he walks in. Oh, and take care of the client until we're finished."

Within minutes Kade sat at Heath's desk, looking between him and Jace, seeing worry etched across both faces.

"Okay. Spit it out. What's going on?"

"J.D. Montalban has been trying to reach you," Heath said.

Kade grabbed his phone, noting several calls from J.D. He'd put it on silent, not wanting calls to interfere with the tour. "Shit," he muttered and looked up. "What'd he say?"

Heath explained the conversation, finishing as Kade's phone rang.

"Taylor."

"Kade, it's J.D. Have you spoken to Heath?"

"Just finished."

"I'm afraid I have more bad news. We've confirmed the Brethren did come your way a week ago. We're checking details now, but it appears they're close to you. No current data on specific activity. My guess is they're lying low, figuring how best to get to you. Have you noted anything at all?"

Kade silently cursed and rubbed the bridge of his nose with his thumb and finger. The worst case situation seemed to be coming true, and a lot faster than he'd guessed.

"Nothing I can tie to the Brethren. Tell me the rest."

"Johnson is working to get an okay to send several of us out your way." DEA Special Agent in Charge Dennis Johnson had been Kade's boss and headed up the San Diego office. Once the man set his teeth into something he didn't let go. "He's getting stonewalled and you know how that pisses him off. I'll wager at least Clive and I will be coming your direction within days."

"Got it." Kade would need to get prepared to trigger his own plans.

"I don't like what I think you're thinking. Tell me." J.D. had known Kade and Nesto for years, hung with them between assignments, and considered both close friends. "You've got to talk to me, bro. I can't have your back if you don't."

Kade walked to the window, turning his back to Heath and Jace. "I'll have to get back to you."

"I won't wait long."

"Got it." Kade hung up, turning to face his uncles. "They're here."

******

"I did have a wonderful time, Dylan. You have a great group of friends." Amber walked down the hall to her office, holding the phone to her ear while juggling an armload of files. "Sure. Coffee tomorrow morning sounds great. Where? Perfect. I'll see you then."

She pushed into her office, dropping the files on her desk, and opening her blinds. The day started out clear and cloudless, with a bite in the air. According to her ex-Marine neighbor, snow should be coming any day. Not a lot, but enough to slow you down.

Amber wondered where Eric was at that moment, wishing he were here in the office, where she had a chance to run into him throughout the day. Funny how she'd grown used to seeing him in the halls, grabbing coffee, or in meetings. Each time, without fail, her chest tightened and the butterflies she'd come to expect fluttered in her stomach. She'd been a fool to think she could work around him and remain untouched.

The phone on her desk rang, pulling her from her thoughts. She glanced at the extension and grabbed the receiver.

"Hello, Heath. Sure. I'll be right there." She grabbed her notebook and pen, then hurried to his office. The urgency in his voice concerned her only a little. He always seemed to have one urgent situation or another for her to tackle since she'd started. She pushed the door open, surprised to find Jace and Kade at the table.

"Have a seat, Amber. We've got something to discuss with you."

Her stomach clenched at the severe tone of Heath's voice and the tension she saw on his face. Her eyes darted between the three men as she lowered herself into a chair.

"You know a little about my situation, correct?" Kade asked her.

"Only what you and Brooke have told me. Why?"

"It seems the object of our concern is closer to Fire Mountain than we thought." He pushed a file toward her. "Go head. Take a look."

She took the manila folder, then hesitated, looking up at Kade.

"It's all right. Nothing gruesome."

Amber opened the file to see several photographs. She looked through them once, then started over, taking more time on each one. All were of men wearing what she knew to be club colors.

"The photos are members of Satan's Brethren, the club I rode with while on assignment with the DEA. This one," he pointed to a grainy image of a lone man with long hair and beard, an almost feral smile on his face, "is Robbie Moran. He took over leadership of the club when his father, Sonny, was arrested. Note his jacket. His cut, or vest, has the same colors on the back. On this one," he pointed to another photo, "is an SBMC tat. The initials refer to Satan's Brethren Motorcycle Club. Most of the brothers have this tattooed somewhere on their body. These men are Robbie's top two bodyguards. This one is Swinger and this is Joker. Don't let their smiles and good looks fool you. Both will kill on an order from Robbie and won't lose any sleep over it." He pierced her with his deep green eyes. "And that includes women."

Amber swallowed and tried to clear the dryness in her throat. "Why are you showing me these?"

"You need to know how to identify them. I've given the same photos to all the others—Brooke, Lainey, Cassie, Annie, Caroline, and the men. It's part of what I planned to review with you this weekend when we met again for training, but the urgency has escalated. I felt it couldn't be put off."

She sat back, a shaky hand pushing a few stray strands of hair away from her eyes. "You know you're scaring me."

"I wish I could tell you it wasn't my intent, but it is. You need to burn these images into your head, study the pictures, and learn to identify the colors. If you see anyone who resembles these men, or wears clothing with these emblems, get in touch with me right away."

"Should I follow them?"

"No!" Kade, Heath, and Jace said in unison.

"Oookay…" her voice trailed off as she lowered her head to look over the pictures again.

"You are not to go after or follow them—under any circumstances. The information and training is for defensive use only. What I've shown you and the others is as much as I can provide on short notice. I'd hoped to have more time or that the intel about the gang coming after me would prove false."

Heath leaned in, resting his arms on the table. "We won't think any less of you if you resign, leave the area. Plus, it might be the smartest move. No one should have to start with a company then find themselves in the middle of something like this. When it's over, you'll be welcomed back."

Until Heath mentioned it, the thought of resigning hadn't occurred to her. His suggestion held little temptation now.

"Thank you for offering, but I'm staying. You can use one more set of eyes, not one less." She turned her attention back to Kade. "What else can I do to help?"

"You're doing all you can. I'll be in touch with everyone else to give them a heads-up."

Amber picked up the folder and stood. "I know this is difficult for each of you. Please let me know if there's anything else I can do—anything."

They nodded before Kade spoke again. "Be aware we may get to the point where you'll need an escort to and from your place."

"But—"

"There's a good chance of it, all right. Just be prepared." Kade watched her leave then picked up his phone. "Eric, I'm here with Heath and Jace. We need to talk."

Chapter Thirteen

"So the rumors are true." Amber sat at the bar between her kitchen and living room in her apartment, sipping coffee before leaving for the office. It had been a couple of days since her meeting with Heath, Jace, and Kade, and she still hadn't quite come to terms with the full implications or dangers.

"Definitely true. I got to work about an hour ago. My supervisor wanted to see me right away. She gave me an envelope which included my notice and information on a severance package." Dana took a shaky breath, still in shock from the news. She thought she'd prepared herself—guess not.

"When is your last day?"

"Today," she choked out, collapsing into her desk chair. "Perfect, huh? She said they don't need my services any longer and I should use the time to find something else."

"And severance?" Amber felt miserable for her closest friend. She knew the feeling of being tossed out as if you didn't matter and all your time with the company meant nothing.

"Three months, plus they'll pay my medical for that long. Oh, and I get my vacation pay." The line went silent for a moment before Dana spoke up again. "Well, I need to pack up. I know I need to keep searching for a new job in Denver, but what I want to do is take a break. Maybe I'll just get a waitress job. Decent hours, good tips." She laughed, but Amber could tell it pained Dana to leave a job she loved.

"Call me tonight. We can talk about you coming out here for a while." Amber cringed as soon as the words were out, knowing Fire Mountain was the last place Dana should be right now.

"That may be the best thing I've heard since waking up this morning. I'll call you tonight."

Amber set down her phone and finished her coffee. Maybe she could take a trip to Cold Creek, Colorado where Cam ran the MacLaren bucking bronc business. He'd invited her out and it was just a few hours east to Denver.

She grabbed her coat and purse, knowing she'd never leave Fire Mountain right now, not with the MacLarens and Sinclairs dealing with such a serious threat. She and Dana would have to keep in touch by phone and email. She'd go through her contacts to see if anyone might have something for Dana, a friend who felt much more like a sister.

Amber pushed the key into the ignition as her phone rang. She looked at the caller ID, seeing it was Eric.

"Are you back?" she asked.

"Not until this weekend. I hope I'm not interrupting you."

"No. Just leaving for the office. What's up?"

"I wanted to check to see how Jillian is doing. If you're aware of anything she needs from me."

"I thought the two of you talked every day? Do you have some concerns?"

"We talk and all seems fine, no real concerns. I'd like your input." Eric rested against the headboard of his hotel bed, having no worries at all about Jillian, but needing to hear Amber's voice. He'd never admit to it, though.

She sat in her car and smiled. "Jillian's bright, resourceful, and pretty much a perfectionist. I think she also has a crush on you."

He pushed straight up, holding the phone tight to his ear. "What? Not a chance. I hardly know her."

"I didn't imply anything, just letting you know. I'm certain the crush will pass once she gets to know you." She bit back a snicker.

Eric didn't respond, making Amber wonder if he'd heard her.

"Have you said anything to her?" he asked in an odd tone.

Amber's brows drew together in confusion. "About what?"

"Us." He stretched out the word, his voice low and smooth.

Her mood changed from fanciful to somber. "No, I've said nothing to anyone. I wanted to talk about it more, but since you're asking, are you certain it's what you want, to try again?" She felt certain he could hear the hard thudding of her heart, which felt almost painful in her chest.

Frustration seeped through him. He didn't believe he could've been more clear about his feelings. "Damn straight I'm certain. I love you and want you in my life—always."

"All right." Her voice came out as a whisper.

Eric fumbled the phone, finally dropping it and scrambling to grab it. "What did you say?"

She let out a breath, her heart racing. "I said yes. Let's try again."

He drew in a breath, not quite believing what he'd heard. He sure as hell wouldn't upset karma by admitting it. "That's good, Amber. Real good." His voice came out rough and full of emotion.

"There's something you need to know, though."

Eric felt his heart seize. He steeled himself before asking. "What?"

"I love you and I'm scared to death about it."

Sweet Jesus, he thought, and fell back onto the bed. She'd almost given him a full on heart attack. He closed his eyes, thanking God for this second chance.

"I'm scared too, babe. We'll just work through this together. That's all I know to do because ignoring it sure hasn't worked."

She laughed at his comment. "No, it sure hasn't."

"I should be back home about eight o'clock Friday night and I'll come right over."

"I'll have dinner ready. See you then."

"And, Amber?"

"Yes?"

"I'm staying the night."

******

"How's Blake doing?" Heath and Jace walked to the parking lot Friday afternoon. It had been a long week and threatened to be an even longer weekend given the danger hanging over the family.

"He's at the house, restless, and ready to head back to school. Given what's happening, I think it's a good idea. The doctor wants him to stay a few more days, then I'm putting him on a plane."

"What's Caroline say?"

"She agrees and wants him away from Fire Mountain." Jace pulled his truck keys from his pocket. "I think we should send all the girls away. I don't like putting them at risk."

"Agreed. We have the two condos in the valley sitting empty. There's enough room for all of them, including Amber." Heath lowered himself into the sports car he'd recently purchased, already thinking he may have made a mistake. His tall frame didn't quite fit in the tight interior, plus his wide boots kept hanging up on the small accelerator pedal. "I'll speak to Annie tonight and call you."

"I'll talk to Caroline. What about the others?" Jace asked.

"Probably should go through the boys, let them explain it."

"Coward."

"Damn straight," Heath replied as he closed the door and started the engine.

He followed Jace onto the street, trailing him to the highway, and turning toward the ranch. A couple miles down he spotted a group of motorcycles parked at the Crossing, the same place where Eric had been hassled. He slowed, noticing Jace doing the same thing before taking a quick right and pulling into the lot. Heath followed him, parking next to his brother.

Jace climbed down, casting a stern look at Heath. "I need a beer."

"I'm with you."

They took a seat at the only empty table, ordered a couple of beers and sat back, their eyes scanning the room.

"Heath, Jace, thought I saw you walk in." Sheriff Tip Andrews shook one hand, then the other.

"Have a seat, Tip. Something we want to talk to you about." Heath pulled out a chair.

"Figured I would've already heard from you." Tip waved for a beer. "What do you know?"

"Nothing more than what Kade told you earlier this week. Wish we knew where they're holed up or if it was a mistake and they've left the area." Heath sipped his beer, letting his gaze settle on three bikers sporting leather jackets without colors. The leather seemed almost too clean as if all three had purchased the gear recently.

"I've got my deputies scouring the area. So far, nothing. The witnesses who saw the gang at a gas stop between the valley and here a couple weeks ago swear they were headed our way—one even mentioned Fire Mountain. I talked to them myself. My guess? They shucked their colors and rode in a couple at a time. Somehow they already had a safe house identified and are staying there, out of sight."

Tip retired as a Marine master sergeant a few years before, winning the sheriff's election not long after returning to his hometown. He'd played football in Fire Mountain and become something of a local legend. No one seemed surprised at his success in the election. Some called him a no-nonsense, hardnosed, leatherneck—to his face. Tim would let out a robust *Oorah!*, agreeing with them one hundred percent. The crime rate in the county had halved since he took over.

"You recognize those three at the bar?" Heath nodded toward the bikers he'd been watching with the clean jackets.

"No, but I'd sure like to get those jackets off 'em. I'm almost certain we'd find tattoos to help identify their club."

"If we wait long enough, they may trip themselves up." Heath finished his beer and signaled for another.

"You may want to slow down on those, Heath. Hate to have to detain you for being over the limit." Tip grinned, only half joking.

"I'm nowhere near my limit, but I'll concede the point. You still have your boys searching for where the club is staying?"

"Twenty-four-seven. As long as no emergencies pop up, the deputies are hunting. Got two of them outside in plain clothes ready to follow the boys at the bar when they leave. Who knows..." Tip's voice trailed off as the bartender yelled something to one of the men standing close to the bikers. "Well, well. We might just get a crack at those boys sooner than we thought." He stood and took a few steps toward the bar, watching as one of the bikers pushed the man away.

"We aren't looking for trouble. Why don't you just back off," one of the bikers said, trying to maintain calm.

The man wouldn't listen and took a threatening step forward, a belligerent glint in his eyes.

"Harry, why don't you do as the man asked and back off?" Tip hated to break it up and lose his chance to see what was hidden under those leather jackets. He hated even more having a neighbor carried off to the hospital.

"Tip's right, Harry." One of his friends took him by the arm and pulled him toward their table, pushing him into a chair. "We're good, Tip."

He continued toward the bar, looking for an opening.

"Don't know as I've seen you in here before. You boys from the area?" Tip asked, leaning against the bar.

"Passing through. May stay a day or two, nothing more." The tallest and meanest looking responded. "No crime is it?"

"Not in my book, but it depends on what you do while you're here. Staying at a local motel?" he pressed.

"Don't have a place yet. Know of one?" His cold stare emphasized eyes holding no compassion. Lifeless is the word that came to Tip's mind.

"We've got several just west of here. Follow the highway. You can't miss them."

"Thanks. We'll do that." He turned his back to Tip, finished his beer, and threw some money on the bar. "Let's get out of here."

Tip watched them leave, knowing his men would follow and keep him posted. He made his way back to Heath and Jace, sinking into a chair while pulling out his phone.

"You got them. Keep me posted. Oh, and let me know which way they head."

"Anything?" Jace asked.

"Nope. Say they're passing through, but I don't buy it. I pointed them west, toward town for a motel. We'll see if that's the way they head." He answered his phone. "I'm not surprised. Yeah, keep following them." He looked up. "They're heading east. Either they're leaving the area or they lied and already have a place to stay."

Heath pushed from the table. "Time for me to head out. Call Jace or me if you learn anything. We're about ready to send the women out of town. I'd like to give them better news than that."

"I hear you. I'll be in touch."

Jace followed Heath outside, Tip close behind. He'd head home and wait to hear from his deputies. He sure wanted to provide his friends with something positive before long.

Chapter Fourteen

Amber couldn't clam down. She'd left the office early, stopped by the grocery store, gotten dinner ready, then changed clothes three times. She'd limited herself to one glass of wine, wanting to have all her senses about her when Eric arrived.

She'd briefly thought of stopping at Victoria's Secret the day before, then changed her mind. The last thing she wanted was to jinx the night. They'd take it slow, see what happened. Forgetting her earlier resolution, she grabbed the bottle of chilled wine and poured half a glass, sipping it as fear began to knot inside her.

She'd felt like a teenager after their phone call, remaining almost giddy throughout the day. Then she'd stop herself, afraid they'd discover the love they once shared had died and couldn't be reclaimed. Doubt would overtake her, then she'd get a text from him saying he loved her and couldn't wait until tonight, and her fear would subside. She'd brought the glass of wine to her lips when the sound of knocking froze her in place. She set the glass down and walked in slow steps toward the door. She gripped the knob and pulled the door open.

A warm smile lit Eric's eyes as he let his gaze wander over her. "Hi."

"Hi." She clutched her hands in front her, not sure what to do next.

"May I come in?" He lifted a brow.

"Oh, yes." She stepped aside, letting him pass, then closed the door, turning to see his eyes darken as they roamed over her.

He took a step forward, his hand reaching out to send a gentle caress of fingertips down her cheek. He moved closer, letting his hand move behind her neck, drawing her to him.

Her heart tripped as he lowered his head, his mouth covering hers in a heated kiss. Her hands crept up his arms, holding tight as he deepened the kiss. The feel of his lips, warm and insistent, shot waves of heat scorching through her.

He pulled back on a ragged breath, his eyes darkening as they locked with hers.

"If we don't stop now, I swear I'll have you in bed before you can blink," he whispered, his rough voice washing over her. He couldn't mistake the look of hope and love in her eyes as she shook her head slightly and leaned into him. He muttered an oath before lowering his head, pulling her so tight he felt as if their mutual heat fused them together.

His hand splayed low on her back, lifting her to feel his body's response as she sighed into his mouth. His other hand moved between them, opening the first three buttons of her blouse and pushing it open, allowing his lips to trace a line from her mouth, down the soft column of her neck, then lower.

Her hands threaded through his hair, holding him in place, moaning as his lips created magic with each touch. Her head fell back, letting the sensations ripple through her.

Eric pulled back once more, the raging desire sending shockwaves through him. He lifted her into his arms, turning toward the back. "Where?" he asked, his voice hoarse with passion.

"There," she nodded as he walked down the short hallway.

He kicked open the door, taking long strides to the bed, and laying her across it. He looked down at her, his pulse racing at the sight. "God, you're so beautiful. Even more stunning than before." He loosened the buttons of his shirt, pulling it free as he lay beside her, letting a hand move up her thigh. He pulled her toward him, melding them together, and capturing her mouth for another kiss.

She made a low sound of pleasure and drew back. "Make love to me, Eric. Please."

His heart slammed into his chest. There's nothing he wouldn't do for this woman.

"Anything for you, baby," he murmured, his voice thick with need. "I hope you're ready, as this will be a long night."

******

"Thought I'd let you know my deputies lost them." The anger in Tip's voice came through clearly. "They followed the bikers about a mile east. That's when I figure they spotted our car. Bikes split up. Appears my boys chose the wrong one to follow. He ended up going onto the interstate, heading north. That's when my men turned back."

A muscle flickered in Heath's jaw, an indication of the frustration he felt. "Where did they split off?"

"Close to the old church. The one that's been vacant for a couple of years. I should've had

177

more than one car tailing them. Sorry, Heath. Looks like we blew it."

"You did what you could, Tip. Those sorry S.O.B.s have been doing this a long time. They may have made your men before they even pulled onto the highway."

"That supposed to make me feel better?" Tip grumbled. "Because it doesn't."

"Hell, no. It's meant to keep me from punching a hole in the wall. I still can't believe it's happening."

"It's a world few of us understand. You're not supposed to get how they think and operate. Some of the soldiers I've trained have left the Marines and now ride with these outlaw motorcycle clubs. I thought I knew them, understood what made them tick, but I didn't. Still don't. It's a helluva different lifestyle."

"Have you spoken with Kade?" Heath scrubbed his face. He'd never dealt well with what he couldn't control—none of the MacLaren men did. This unknown threat had rocketed his concern to a whole new level.

"No. He's my next call."

"Ask him to call me when you're finished. I think we need to move toward getting the women out of the area." He could imagine the pushback they'd get, but keeping them safe was non-negotiable.

"Agreed. If they do go after Kade, anybody in their way will just be collateral damage." Tip hung up, his words settling in Heath's head.

He mumbled a curse as he went to locate Annie.

******

"Your feet should be a little farther apart. That's good. Now aim and squeeze the trigger." Kade stood behind Amber, so close she could feel his breath fan her cheek. She knew Eric watched from a few feet away, encouraging her with an occasional nod while shooting Kade a warning look.

"Darn it. I missed again." Amber lowered the gun, irritated with her lack of concentration.

Kade set his hands on her hips, moving her just an inch or two and earning himself a low growl from Eric. Kade glanced over his shoulder at him to see his arms crossed, his legs shoulder width apart.

"Sorry, bro, but I need her in the right spot. You want to take over?" He sent Eric a knowing smirk. He'd seen them drive up together, noticed the way they looked—like they'd spent the entire night in bed, together. From where he stood, it was about time.

He glared at his brother-in-law, knowing Kade had a job to do, but still not liking the fact it included putting his hands on Eric's woman. He shook his head at the thought, not quite believing she was his again. There wasn't a chance he'd let her go a second time.

Last night had been explosive. Nothing could've prepared him for her incredible response to his touch. And the passion didn't stop after one time. They'd made love over and over until they'd been too exhausted to do anything except drift into asleep. His body began to harden at the memory. He groaned, adjusting his stance and trying to relieve the discomfort.

"No, you go ahead. You're the pro and I'm just trying to pick up some pointers."

Kade chuckled at the comment. "Right."

Amber looked from one to the other, her brows knitting together.

"Have you ever seen him shoot?" Kade asked. She shook her head. "He's good. Wished we'd had him in Special Ops with us."

She narrowed her eyes at Kade before glancing at Eric, then shrugged to hide her confusion. "I had no idea."

"You ought to ask him about it sometime. Okay, are you ready to continue?"

An hour later they packed up the gear and walked toward the house, watching as Heath came out to greet them.

"Glad you're here. We need to talk if you have time." He directed his request to Kade, then glanced at Eric and Amber. "Annie has sandwiches if you're hungry."

Kade followed Heath into his office while Eric grabbed Amber's hand and walked toward the kitchen. The gesture wasn't lost on Heath.

Kade took a seat and draped an arm over the back of the chair. "Tip told me the two of you spoke and you were aware of the tail. Wish he'd let me know what was going down, I might've been able to help." He'd controlled his anger at being left out of the loop until now. His time in the Army and the DEA had taught him the biggest errors occurred when communication between colleagues ceased. "Shit, Heath. Someone should've called me."

Heath grabbed a couple of waters, tossing one to Kade before twisting his own open and taking a long swallow.

"It went down fast. Jace and I were grabbing beers when Tip joined us. The bikers were already in the bar. Tip had an unmarked car outside with two deputies ready to tail the bikers. We didn't even know about it until the bikers left the bar. You'd never have been able to get there in time." He finished his water and tossed the empty bottle into the trash. "I think it's time to move the girls to the valley."

Kade leaned forward, resting his arms on his knees, rolling the bottle of water between his hands. "They'll fight us. They're a stubborn bunch."

Heath chuckled and took a seat near Kade. "That they are. I think we should call the family together, explain what's happening. Have you heard any more from your contacts? Are they sending anyone out?"

"J.D. called this morning. No word yet, at least not enough to get the go-head from Agent Johnson for him and Clive to come out. J.D. said he'll take vacation time if he has to if this drags on much longer. Clive Nelson's on board with it, also. Both are frustrated. They're certain the Brethren plan to come after me, but the agency isn't convinced enough to cut loose with extra resources. It's as under control here as it would be if I'd agreed to protective custody."

"Did they offer it?" Heath's eyes narrowed on Kade, surprised he hadn't pulled himself out of harm's way.

"I turned them down." Kade stood and paced toward the wall of pictures, focusing on one of Heath, Jace, and Rafe when they were in high school. "I know the Brethren. Protective custody won't work." He turned back toward Heath, his voice hard. "If they can't get to me directly, they'll come after Brooke or any of my family. That's how they operate. Threats, kidnapping, intimidation, torture—whatever it takes to get what they want. I won't make the family the focus of the gang's wrath. I'm better off in the open, trying to draw them out."

"Hell," Heath muttered, rubbing his eyes with the palms of his hands. "What do we do now?"

"Like you said. Bring the family together, get all of it in the open, including the option of protective custody. And try to talk the women into leaving for the valley. When do you want to do this?"

"Everyone will be here tomorrow. We'll do it then."

******

"Are you out of your fuckin' minds?" Swinger grabbed Rookie by the collar and slammed him up against a wall. "I told you to stay put until Joker and I got back. What part of that didn't you assholes get?" He moved his other hand up to wrap around Rookie's windpipe, squeezing until the man almost lost consciousness.

"Enough," Joker said, stepping next to Swinger but not laying a hand on him.

Swinger glanced over, rage burning in his eyes. He dropped the hand from Rookie's neck, then reared back and shot a fist into his jaw, letting him crumble to the ground. He swung toward the others who'd followed Rookie to the bar.

"You get me now?" he growled. "This isn't a fuckin' game. It's real and someone is going to die when it's over. If you sons of bitches aren't up for it, I'll call Robbie, have him send replacements."

"We got you, Swinger. No more trips and no need to contact Robbie." Sledge glanced at Rookie, still out cold on the floor, then back at Swinger. He'd earned full patch status a few months before. No way did he want to be the object of Robbie's anger. Sledge had been the one to draw the deputies to the interstate, where they'd given up and turned back, allowing his brothers to return to the house. "There's no chance the heat knows where we are. None."

"Shut up." Swinger grabbed a beer from the refrigerator and threw one to Joker. "There's no such thing as 'no chance', shithead."

He and Joker had driven onto the ranch a week before, being turned back before they got to the main house. They'd tried again yesterday, picking up a different rental car, wearing plaid shirts and heavy canvas coats. This time they came in another way and followed a narrow dirt road. They'd driven for an hour, spotting nothing before a black SUV pulled in front of them, blocking their path. Swinger made excuses about looking for property they'd heard was on the market, turned the car around, and left.

He chugged the beer all at once, crumpling the can and throwing it in a corner. "I've got to call Robbie. Keep watch." Swinger disappeared into a back room. Robbie picked up on the second ring.

"What's the news?"

"We aren't going to be able to get him on the ranch. Got to grab him when he comes off." Swinger paced back and forth, waiting for his Prez to respond.

Robbie slumped into a chair, thinking through options. Swinger knew more about grabbing targets than anyone in the club. He had a hundred percent record of bringing back or disposing of anyone he tracked.

"What do you suggest?"

"Snatch his old lady. Use her as bait." Swinger grabbed another beer, knowing Robbie needed to ponder this before giving approval. He'd never advocated using women or children unless there was no other choice. His Prez knew if Swinger suggested it, no other option would work.

"If we do this, I want to be there."

"I don't think that's such a good—"

"Did I ask you?"

"No, Robbie, but my job is to keep you safe, out of this kind of shit. You should stay in Texas, out of sight. Let us take care of him."

"Not happening. I got more reason to want the bastard than anyone, and I'll be the one to take care of him."

"Damn it, Robbie. At least tell me you're bringing some brothers to keep watch for you."

"Me and two others. I'll figure out who. Send me a picture of his old lady. I'll let you know when I'll be taking off." Robbie hung up, leaving nothing for Swinger to do except swear.

Chapter Fifteen

"Dress up. I'm taking you out tonight after I take care of some stuff." Eric leaned down to kiss Amber as he slipped into his shirt. They'd come to her place after leaving the ranch and spent the last few hours in bed. It had been the best couple of days he'd had in years—since before they'd split up.

"We don't have to go out. I can cook." She drew her fingertips down his chest, her voice sultry and low.

"Yeah, and end up like last night without food?" His chuckle came out as more of a hiss as his body began to warm.

"You didn't like it?" A slight pout crossed her face as she worked her way toward the belt he'd just buckled. He reached down and stilled her hands.

"You're going to kill me, you know that don't you?" He grinned before wrapping an arm around her and pulling her tight, covering her mouth with his. "God, you make me crazy," he breathed against her lips before pushing her back onto the bed and following her down.

An hour later he pulled onto the street. A quick trip to his place to change clothes, answer emails, and check with Kade, and then drive back to Amber's. He planned to take her to his favorite spot. A place he'd never taken another date. Somehow he'd always known it should be saved for someone special.

He turned off the engine when his phone rang.

"Sinclair," he answered.

"Eric, it's Keith Vance. I've got all the documents together and would like to come out this week to make a presentation about the various properties. Would Wednesday or Thursday work for you?"

Eric pushed open his front door then shoved it closed against the cold wind. "Let me check with a few people. I'd like you to get in front of the leadership. If they aren't available, then we should put it off until they can attend."

"Understood. Let me know as soon as you can. I may bring an associate with me."

"No problem. I'll get back in touch Monday." He hung up then hopped in the shower.

Eric let the hot water sluice over him, thinking of Amber, and growing impatient to see her again as his body responded. He knew the desire and urgency they felt for each other would subside or slow after a few weeks, or months, or if he were lucky, years. Heath and Annie never seemed to grow tired of being around each other. The same with Cam and Lainey, and Trey and Jesse. He chuckled as he thought of Kade and Brooke and the way she'd thrown herself at him in front of the family without any sense of humility. He wanted that—uninhibited passion from Amber for the rest of their lives.

His chest tightened at the thought. They'd just gotten back together, yet he knew without a doubt he never wanted to be without her again. He never believed they'd have a second chance, yet here they were, back together. They were older, perhaps wiser, with more to lose than before. He understood Amber's fear—he felt it, too. If it didn't work this time, he didn't know what he'd do.

Eric stopped at the flower store on the way to Amber's and picked up a dozen red roses. The next stop was for a bottle of her favorite wine. He'd allow her one glass before they left, and even that might be too much if the last twenty-four hours was any indication. Maybe he'd better leave the wine in the truck. Tonight he wished he owned a sports car like Heath's new one. He wanted the best for her.

She opened the door, her eyes growing wide at the sight of the roses Eric held out.

"They're beautiful." Her voice held a gentle softness, which tapped something deep inside of him.

She placed the roses in water then set them in the center of the table before grabbing her phone and taking a picture. Pulling up the image, she walked toward Eric and showed it to him, a proud look on her face.

"What are you gloating about?" He narrowed his eyes at her.

"I'm saving it for those times in the future when you slink into some mysterious man-funk. I'll show this to you. Maybe it will help you to snap out of it."

He shook his head, not quite sure what she meant but liking the part about the future.

"You look beautiful." He pulled her toward him, meaning to give her a quick kiss before leaving for dinner. Instead, he moved his mouth over hers, brushing his lips across hers in soft strokes before deepening the kiss. She sighed as his grip tightened, molding herself to him until he pulled away and rested his forehead against hers.

"You make me forget all sense of time or where I am." His glazed eyes locked on hers, seeing the passion he felt. He almost decided to call off their dinner, swoop her up and take her to bed. She had plenty of food in the refrigerator, all they'd need to get through the night. Then he let out a ragged breath and stepped away.

"I'll help you with your coat. We have a reservation in twenty minutes."

Amber nodded, missing the warmth and feel of his body the moment he stepped away.

He drove through areas of town she'd never seen, taking a winding road up a hillside, and entering a drive almost hidden within the pines. Her eyes widened as they pulled to a stop before a magnificent Victorian mansion.

Lights bathed the intricate details and colors of cream, brown, and russet. A veranda extended across the entire width of the first story and wrapped around two sides. There were balconies on each of the upper stories and as Eric helped Amber out of the truck, she could see four chimneys.

"It's glorious," she whispered and took his arm.

"Wait until you see the inside."

Eric stopped at the ornate double doors and stepped aside for Amber to walk past him. She came to a halt, staring up at the cathedral ceiling, then letting her gaze move lower to see an older woman with a broad smile watching her.

"Good evening, Eric." She walked up to give him a warm hug. "It's been a while. I believe the last time I saw you in here we were celebrating Heath's birthday."

"You have a good memory, Esther." Eric drew Amber toward him. "This is Amber Anderson. Amber, meet Esther Hastings, owner of this fabulous restaurant."

"It's a pleasure, Mrs...."

"Esther, please." She looked at Eric. "I don't believe I've ever seen you bring a date in here."

"Yeah...well..." Eric hesitated, not quite sure how to continue.

"You must be quite special, Amber, for Eric to bring you here." Esther watched as Amber blushed, then smiled, and tightened her grip on Eric's arm. "Now, let me show you to your table."

Their evening couldn't have been better. Esther brought them a special she'd prepared and when Amber thought nothing more would fit in her stomach, Esther carried a beautiful fresh fruit pie to the table, still steaming with a side of ice cream for each.

Eric and Amber stared at each other then laughed. "Any coffee to go with it, Esther?"

"Of course."

Eric waited until they'd finished their dessert before asking what had been on his mind all evening. "How are you feeling so far, about us I mean?"

They'd talked about everything except the one topic which hung between them like the thick fog over the Golden Gate Bridge.

Amber set her fork down and reached across the table, taking his hand. "I think we're doing wonderful. I know it's been a short time and anything might happen, but you should know I want this to work. More than I've ever wanted anything."

A smile lit her face and Eric felt his chest seize. "Me, too," he whispered, his voice thick with emotion. He squeezed her hand, knowing in his heart nothing could pull them apart again. "Let's get out of here."

Amber held his hand and lost herself in her own mental ramblings as Eric drove home. She paid no attention to the direction, looking up only when the truck began to go across a bumpy road. She glanced at him then out the window, disoriented.

"Where are we going?" She looked around, seeing nothing except miles of grassland in the almost moonless night.

"To my place. It's time we made love in my bed." The smile he offered sent shivers through her body as her heart hammered almost violently in her chest. He pulled to a stop in front of a cabin with a view to the valley below.

A few tall pines and scrub oaks dotted the area around the house. In the distance Amber could see lights from other houses.

"The lights over there are from Cam and Lainey's place, and those are from Kade and Brooke's. That," he pointed in a third direction, "is where Heath and Annie live."

"How far away are they?"

"The cabins are about half a mile apart, while the ranch house is closer to a mile away. We drove in from a side road few people know about. I'll show it to you during the day as it's closer when coming from your place."

"You seem to believe I'll be coming here a lot," she teased.

"Unless you move in, which would be the best from my perspective." He locked eyes on her, waiting.

Her breath hitched at the thought. "I think it's worth discussing," she finally said, taking his hand as he led her into the cabin.

He closed the front door behind them, then turned to face her, cupping her face in his hands. "When you're ready, I want you to move in with me. I want you in my bed every night." He placed a soft kiss on her lips and drew back.

"And marriage?"

"Is that a proposal? Because if it is, I accept." His smile broke her nervous reaction at the thought of moving in with him. They'd lived together a brief time in college before the split and her departure for New York. All had gone well. They talked, rarely fought, and became each other's best friend. And their lovemaking...well...had only gotten better. They could do it again, she was certain of it.

******

They woke up Sunday morning to a light dusting of snow and winds strong enough to push you off balance. Breakfast consisted of eggs, toast, and orange juice before Eric scooped her up and carried her back to bed.

"I could get used to this." Eric pulled a strong arm around her and tugged her close, gathering the covers around them.

"Yeah?"

"Oh, yeah."

She could feel his soft breaths fan her cheeks as he placed kisses behind her ear and softly nipped at the lobe. "Do you still want children?"

His question took her by surprise, although she didn't know why. They'd talked of a family many times while engaged. Eric loved children, and so did Amber. Her thoughts hadn't changed over the years.

"If I can have them with you, yes."

He lifted her and set her on top of him before she had a chance to protest, his gaze boring into her.

"Marry me, Amber." He put a finger to her lips when they began to part. "I love you, always have. Waiting won't change how I feel and I don't believe we'll find any dark secrets about the other neither can live with." He grabbed both her hands, touching his lips to them. "The wedding can be months off if it will make you feel better. But I want a ring on your finger now, so everyone knows you're mine."

She stared down at him, eyes wide, not knowing quite what to say. Her heart pounded, causing heat to course through her and a flush of warmth on her face. She hadn't been prepared for this—not yet. A lump formed in her throat, which she forced herself to swallow.

"You don't think it's too soon?"

"Not at all." His eyes narrowed on hers. "I can't imagine living without you. If you're afraid I'll change my mind, I won't. Not ever. You're it for me, Amber."

Her eyes darted around the room as she tried to focus on what to do. She loved him, had since they'd been in high school. Years had gone by and her feelings had become stronger. Like Eric, she couldn't imagine a future without him in it. Amber took a breath and placed her palms on his chest, feeling his heart pounding as rapidly as her own. She caught her lower lip between her teeth before releasing it and running her tongue across her lips.

"All right."

Eric shot upright, not quite believing her answer. "What?"

"I said, yes. I love you and I'll marry you, but with one condition."

He stilled, waiting.

"The end of summer." She cleared her throat. "I want an August wedding."

A smile broke across Eric's face as he recalled a similar discussion years before.

"That's when we planned to marry before, in August." He wrapped his arms around her, holding her tight, not wanting to let her go. "August it is, sweetheart."

Chapter Sixteen

"All right, who's missing?" Heath asked as everyone gathered in the great room before Sunday dinner. Even Rafe had flown in from Montana for business and to see Mitch and Kade. Heath had to hand it to him—his brother was making a hell of an effort to reunite with the family he'd turned his back on years before and the son he'd known nothing about. Bringing his Montana family into the fold might take longer. At least Mitch seemed to be doing his part to build a bridge with Kade.

"Just Eric," Annie said, putting a hand on Heath's shoulder at the same time the door burst open and Eric walked inside holding Amber's hand.

"Sorry, we're late." He walked up to his mother, giving her a hug and kiss, then shook Heath's hand, never dropping his grip on Amber.

The room fell silent, everyone noticing how the two looked at each other and waited. Eric draped an arm around her shoulders, then held up her left hand, showing off the beautiful diamond ring on her finger. The same one she'd worn years before.

"I know this will seem sudden, but Amber and I are back together. She's agreed to marry me." He leaned down to kiss her as the room broke out in chaos.

Brooke screamed and shot out of her chair, wrapping Amber in a death hug, then turning to Eric. "It's about time the two of you got your act together." She grinned then pulled him into her arms.

Eric felt a hand on his shoulder and turned to see Heath standing next to him. "Congratulations, son. I think you've made a wise decision."

"Thanks. I know we need to talk about how this will play out at work—"

"We'll make it work. Don't worry about it."

"Congratulations, bro." Kade held out his hand, Cam and Mitch right next to him. The four formed a circle, Mitch handing him a beer. A few feet away, Amber found herself in a similar circle of MacLaren and Sinclair women.

The celebratory mood lasted through dinner until Heath stood, cleared his throat, and looked at Kade. His somber expression moved from one person to another until the room fell silent.

"We've gotten some wonderful news from Eric and Amber today, and I hate to dampen the festivities, but the situation we're all aware of has escalated. Kade is the best person to explain what's happening and provide some answers."

Kade didn't stand, preferring to lean forward and place his arms on the table.

"All indications point to Satan's Brethren being in the area. From what we know, a group of them rode from San Diego through Yuma, passing through the valley and stopping for gasoline about ten miles east of here. Sheriff Andrews and Chief Towers have their people actively looking for where the bikers are staying. So far, nothing." He cast a look at Brooke before proceeding, noting the concern on her face. "You've all been given packets with photos of what their colors look like and the faces of those I believe will be looking for me. I've provided as much training in self-protection as I can at this point and I want there to be no doubt it is to be used for nothing except defending yourself."

He pushed from the table and walked to the bar, which separated the kitchen from the eating area, and leaned against it. "What I'm asking is for everyone in this room to be on alert, watch for anyone wearing the colors, asking questions, or acting suspicious. Do not confront them under any circumstances."

"What about the DEA? Aren't they sending anyone to help?" Mitch had a hard time believing the agency would let the bikers get this close to a key witness in the prosecution of Sonny Morgan.

"Not yet, but I expect to have at least agents Nelson and Montalban in Fire Mountain soon—within days if my guess is right. Sheriff Andrews and Chief Towers have their people on high alert. If they spot anything, they've agreed to contact the DEA, Heath, and me right away."

"What about putting you in some kind of protective custody?" Rafe stood, pacing toward a window and peering outside. Kade's father had remained silent until now, although he'd been made aware of the danger during his last trip to Fire Mountain.

"They offered. I refused."

"Why?" Rafe asked, his voice hard and intense.

Kade drew in a deep breath, knowing his decision would anger some of the family.

"I've lived in the club. Satan's Brethren are as bad as it gets in the one-percent biker world."

"And you fit in the group for a long time without them knowing." Mitch still had a hard time reconciling what he knew of the vicious biker gang to the fact his brother had become a full patch member of the club.

Kade narrowed his eyes on his half-brother. "Yes, I did. I'm proud of what came from my assignment, not what I had to do to make it happen." He shifted his stance, once more glancing at Brooke then back at the others. "As far as protective custody and the club, no one is safe. If I'm in the wind, they'll set their sights on a family member, kidnap them, and use them as leverage. I won't let that happen."

"In the wind?" Cam asked.

"Disappear, such as in WITSEC, the Witness Protection program. The women would be their target of choice, Brooke first, then the others if I disappear. If I stay, they'll be focused on me, not my family." He looked around the room, making eye contact with each person, people he'd come to love and trust.

"What exactly are you telling us?" Rafe asked, certain he already knew.

"I plan to make myself visible. Ride alone, make it easy for them to spot me."

"The hell you will." Rafe's voice thundered through the room. "I'll not have my son setting himself up to be taken by murderers. Not a chance."

Silence enveloped the room at the apparent standoff between father and son. Rafe glared at Kade, daring him to defend his decision.

"Look, there's got to be a way to work through this." Mitch stood and walked toward his father. Rafe ignored him, continuing to focus his attention on Kade.

Kade pushed away from the counter. "When I said alone, what I should have included was that Nelson and Montalban will have my back, as will local sheriff's deputies and police. My trips will be orchestrated." He stepped toward his father. "I'll be covered."

"I still don't like it," Rafe ground out, crossing his arms over his chest. "They had your back last summer and you almost died."

"That was different. I didn't know they were following me. This time I will and we'll be in communication."

Eric squeezed Amber's hand and pushed from the table. "I'm riding with you."

"Me too," Mitch added. "Not that I don't trust the law, but no one will have your back the way family will. And don't argue with us on this."

Kade's throat closed up and he pursed his lips, not sure how to respond. "Look, I appreciate you wanting to look after me, but it won't work. I need to be an easy target for them. The two of you will just complicate things."

"So, we confront complications all the time," Eric responded. "The deal is, we ride together or we tie you up and leave you someplace until this is over. Your choice."

"You're not law enforcement," Kade countered.

"Neither are you," Eric reminded him. Kade had left the DEA months before. He was as much of a civilian as any of them.

Kade cursed under his breath, although he was pretty sure everyone heard.

"Guess I'd better get a bike so I can ride along." Cam drained his beer and set the empty bottle on the table.

"Not a chance. You're in charge of getting the women settled in our condos in the valley." Heath's comment set off a chain of female objections even he wasn't prepared to handle.

Brooke, Cassie, Amber, and Lainey jumped from their seats, protesting any suggestion they leave the area. Brooke walked toward Kade, telling him point blank she wouldn't be leaving.

Annie lifted her brows at Heath, telling him without words what she thought of his idea.

"This isn't open for discussion. We need the women where we know they'll be safe." Eric's eyes were hard, yet pleading with Amber to understand.

"Perhaps we're not making ourselves clear," Amber responded, fisted hands on her hips. "Unless you're prepared to physically restrain us, we won't be going anywhere." She glared up at him. "Do we understand each other now?"

"Shit," Eric murmured and scrubbed a hand over his face.

Heath cleared his throat, accepting the men had lost this round in the battle. He wasn't yet ready to concede the war. He wanted Annie and the other women safe, no matter the anger that would flow in the aftermath.

Chapter Seventeen

Silence fell between Eric and Amber as they drove toward her apartment. She'd agreed to pack some clothes, her computer and work files, then spend the night at his place. The original monthly rental contract she'd reluctantly agreed to sign now worked to her advantage.

Eric reached over and grabbed her hand, settling it on his thigh. "You okay?"

She snorted. "Of course. Nothing like a death threat hanging over Kade to cap off our engagement announcement." She watched as Eric lifted her hand, kissing it and the ring.

"What can I say? Life with the MacLaren and Sinclair families is always filled with surprises."

"And I don't want to miss a one." She shot him a smile then rested her head on the seat back and closed her eyes.

"Hey, is that your phone?" Eric asked.

Amber realized she must have drifted off as she fumbled for the phone in her purse. "Hello."

"Hi. It's Dana. Is this a good time to talk?"

"Of course. What's up?"

"I have a surprise for you. I'm on the interstate about forty miles from Fire Mountain. Can I crash at your place?"

Amber's jaw dropped at the announcement. "Uh...yes...of course, you can stay at my place. Do you know how to get here?"

"I've got my GPS locked and loaded. My guess is I'll arrive in less than an hour."

Amber laughed. "Okay. We'll wait for you at my place."

"We?"

Amber glanced at Eric, who lifted his brows at her and grinned. "I'll explain when you get here." She slipped the phone in her purse as Eric pulled into the complex, parked, and turned toward her.

"And that was..."

"Dana. My best friend. She lost her job in Denver and decided to surprise me by driving out for a visit. She's less than an hour away. Sorry."

"No worries. She can stay at your place and we'll sleep at the cabin." He smiled, trailing the back of his hand down her cheek. "Come on. We'll get your stuff packed before she arrives."

"Eric..."

He turned back toward her. "I'm not sleeping without you when you've just agreed to marry me."

"It wouldn't be right walking out on Dana her first night in town. I'd feel horrible."

"Tell you what. We'll ask her." He winked and walked around the truck to open her door.

It took less than thirty minutes to pack what Amber needed. She still wasn't sure she'd leave and wouldn't make a decision until Dana arrived. It had been a couple of months since they'd seen each other and she didn't want to waste a moment of their time. She didn't want to sleep without Eric in her bed either.

She grabbed her phone on the second ring.

"I'm outside. Okay to come up?" Dana asked.

"I'll be right out." Amber headed toward the parking lot, Eric right behind. "Hey!" She ran up to Dana and wrapped her arms around her. "What a surprise."

"I had the time and thought, why not? It took about ten minutes to pack and twelve hours to make the drive." Dana looked up, spotting Eric for the first time, and stepped back. "And who is this?" Her unapologetic gaze wandered up and down Eric. She nodded in approval.

"Eric Sinclair." He reached out his hand to Dana. "Amber's fiancé."

She shot a look at Amber. "No shit?"

"Yes." Amber held up her hand and wiggled her fingers, showing off the stunning ring.

"Oh my God. I can't believe it!" She wrapped Amber in another hug. "I think I'll need a glass of wine while you explain all that's happened." She looked at Eric. "Medicinal purposes only, of course."

Eric chuckled, grabbed her bag, and followed them into the apartment.

An hour later Dana began to fade. One yawn led to another, then another until her eyes were drifting shut. "I guess I'd better get to bed. Where should I sleep?"

"Well, my room is down the hall and the bath is next to it. Um...Eric and I thought, perhaps..."

Dana pushed up from the sofa, hugged Amber, then grabbed her bag. "Get out of here. I'm too tired to care where you sleep." She winked at Eric then turned back to Amber. "Call me tomorrow when you get a break."

"How about lunch tomorrow?" Amber asked.

"Perfect. Just let me know where."

******

"I like her, except her timing couldn't be worse."

"I know, but what could I do? She'd already made the drive. At least she can have the apartment to herself." Amber tried to hide a yawn and failed. "Sorry. It's been a couple of long, sleep-deprived nights. What do you suggest I tell her about what's going on with the family?"

He liked the way she included herself in *the family.*

"I'd like to leave her out of it altogether, but we should discuss it with Kade, Heath, and Jace. They might tell you to send her back to Denver. No sense having someone else in danger." He kept glancing in his mirrors and taking particular care as they approached each intersection. There'd been a couple of riders. None displaying colors or acting as if his truck was anything special. Still, he had a sense of foreboding he couldn't seem to shake. "I wish you and the other women would leave for the valley. I know you don't want to, but I'd rather we focus on the threat against Kade, and not have to worry about you and the other women."

211

Amber clasped her hands in her lap. She understood Eric's concern and his logic seemed sound, however, she felt the same as Brooke and the others. They'd never be able to stay away knowing Kade, Eric, or any of the men were in danger. She reached over and grabbed his hand.

"I know you're worried and want us safe. Try to understand we're in the same position. Would you be able to sit around and wait for word if the situation was reversed?"

Eric shook his head, knowing she was right. He'd be climbing the walls. More than that, he would refuse to leave in the first place, same as the women.

"I'll back off for now, but fair warning. If the threats materialize, I'll be the first to pack you up and get you out of town. And that's a promise, Amber." He parked next to his cabin and grabbed her bags from the back.

They walked inside, Eric watching as Amber set her computer on the table then turned toward him. A smile crossed her face before she took a couple of steps and stopped before him.

She wrapped her arms around his neck, pulling him down to fuse her mouth with his. The bags fell from his grip, his hands moving to her hips, grasping her tight as he deepened the kiss.

His hands massaged their way up and down her back, eliciting a soft moan. "Perhaps we should finish this in bed," he said against her lips. "Did I ever mention how good I am at giving massages?"

She opened her eyes. "Do I want to know who you practiced on?" Her voice sounded thick with need.

He shook his head. "Trust me, you'll enjoy it. Come on." He claimed her mouth again before resting an arm around her shoulders. "You sure we have to wait until August?"

She looked up at him and smiled. "Perhaps we should put that up for negotiation. Can we discuss it more in the morning?"

"Whenever you want, babe."

******

"We're set for Thursday afternoon, Keith. I have a lunch meeting but our marketing director will meet you and your associate." Eric grabbed a pen and jotted down some information. "Sounds good. I'll see you then."

He hung up and sent a meeting notice to those attending the meeting with Keith regarding possible properties. He shot a quick email to Amber, confirming she'd be taking

Keith and his associate to lunch then escorting them to the meeting.

They'd crawled out of bed about seven that morning—later than normal for both on a Monday. No matter how he vowed to keep his hands off her and let her sleep, he found himself stroking her arms, her back, her stomach until she woke and let him make love to her again. If they didn't get some sleep tonight, they'd be worthless. He looked up at a soft knock and saw his door opening.

"Hey." Amber walked in, carrying a stack of folders "I never had a chance to show you the updated layout for the brochures. I can leave them if this isn't a good time."

He walked over and shut the door then drew her into his arms. "Now is great." His mouth settled on hers. Heat built quickly until Amber broke the kiss, pushed his shoulders, and shot him a warning grin.

"You know, anyone could walk in."

"And?"

"You're incorrigible," she laughed and set the files on his desk, pointing to his chair. "We have about thirty minutes before your meeting with Jillian."

Amber walked him through the recommended changes, pointing out the reasons for each one. If the design worked, she planned to convert existing brochures for the other companies to a similar scheme.

"You can see that the colors change for each property, and of course, the logo for the particular development will differ. The MacLaren Enterprises logo won't change from one project to the next."

Eric studied all the layouts, impressed more than he'd expected to be with her work. They'd reviewed drafts in previous meetings and the final layouts showed she'd taken his comments seriously. He pulled a sample forward, then another, finding nothing he wanted to change.

He pushed the files toward her. "These are exceptional. Much better than the other material I've seen from competing developments. Have you shown these to anyone else?"

"Other than Jillian, you're the first to see them." Amber had been a ball of nerves all morning, concerned how Eric would take the updated designs. He'd been the one to develop the previous package. And although he'd done quite well with them, selling out their properties at a faster rate than other similar developments, she felt certain they could be better.

He opened one folder. "Something else is different, yet I can't put my finger on it. There's a different feel to the graphics. You did work with the design firm used by the company, right?"

"Well...not exactly."

"You didn't use the firm Heath put in place a few years ago?"

"No. I used someone else. I've worked with her before and always had great results. Imaginative, professional, within budget..." her voice trailed off.

"Dana?"

Her eyes widened in surprise. "How'd you know?"

Eric shook his head as a smile broke across his face. He picked up an old brochure, placing it next to the new design, then started to laugh.

"What's so funny?"

"This is going to come as quite a surprise to Heath, but mom is going to love it."

"Are you going to let me in on it or let me be blindsided when I show these to Heath?"

"Oh, trust me, I'll be there when you show these to him. The designer we've been using is an old girlfriend of his—or as close to a girlfriend as Heath had before he met mom. He's kept her on, even though few of us thought she worked at the level needed."

"Did you tell him your thoughts earlier?"

"Oh, yeah. Guess he couldn't cut her loose. He's a pretty loyal guy, which is good and bad. Anyway, this may be just what we need to push her out and open the door for someone else." His eyes lit up at the thought. "And mom is going to love it."

Mitch pushed the door open and walked in, followed by Kade. "Sorry to interrupt, but Heath's called a meeting and wants you in it." He glanced at Amber. "Acquisition stuff. I'm sure you'll be brought in later," he said, switching his eyes to Eric. "We'll see you in his office."

"I'm right behind you." Eric grabbed his notebook. "Dinner?" he asked as they stepped into the hall.

"Your mom's. She called this morning and I told her about Dana." She shrugged, knowing Eric wouldn't have turned down her offer to make dinner either. "I'll pick up Dana and head over."

"Let her follow you." He leaned down and gave her a quick kiss on the cheek. "You're staying with me, remember?"

She watched him walk down the hall, noticing again how well he filled out his jeans. A shiver ran through her as she remembered the feel of his legs entwined with hers. Had it been just days since they'd given it another shot?

"Did he like the changes?" Jillian asked, coming to a halt next to Amber.

"He sure did. Come on, I have a new project you can help with while he meets with Heath."

******

"Close the door, Mitch. Kade, you want to bring us up to date?" Heath asked.

"I've heard from Agent Montalban. Robbie Morgan and three of his men left Appleton, Texas this morning. They're traveling west."

"Where's Appleton?" Eric asked as a knot formed in his stomach.

"Far east side, near the Louisiana border."

"Montalban have any idea how long it will take for them to get here?" Eric leaned forward, arms resting on the table.

"If they take a direct route, stopping to sleep and eat, about three days. J.D. will keep me posted, but we need to plan for the possibility he's coming here. Wish I had better news."

"It's not your fault, Kade." Rafe had made the decision to stay in Fire Mountain until the threat passed.

"If I hadn't met Brooke, married her—"

218

"Don't go there," Eric cut in. "You're the best thing that's ever happened to her. Besides, we deal with what we have and right now we have a heads-up. What do we do with the information?"

"J.D. already spoke with Sheriff Andrews and Chief Towers. They're working together to set up road blocks if Morgan does come this way. J.D. and Clive Nelson are on their way here. Ernesto Salgado is trying to get some time off, but I can't count on it. The Marshal Service is short-handed right now. The soonest Morgan will arrive is Thursday. He'll need time to formulate a plan. My guess is the first opportunity Robbie will have to make his move is early next week."

"The women?" Eric asked.

"Getting them to leave for the valley is a wasted effort." Heath shook his head in frustration. "I've been told to not even ask again."

"Then we have to find a way to protect them while keeping watch for Robbie." Eric knew how stubborn his mom could be. In fact, none of the women were shy about sharing their thoughts, and all were firm in their decision to stay. "Amber is the only one with an apartment away from the ranch. I can get her to stay with me, but now we have a new issue. Her friend, Dana, drove in last night from Denver.”

“Jesus, Eric—” Mitch started.

“Nothing I could do, Mitch. Amber didn’t even know she was coming.”

“We’ll set her up in another cabin while she’s here. How much should we tell her, Kade?” Jace asked.

Kade looked at Eric. “How do you think she’ll handle what’s going on?”

“First impression? She’ll do fine. We can give her a choice—stay or head home. Of course, I’d rather she leave. One less woman to worry about.” Eric tossed his pen on the table.

“All women will be staying on the ranch. We’ll close up all roads except the main entrance. Women come and go in a group of no less than two, and one of us accompanies them. No one drives out alone and we know where everyone is at all times. No exceptions. J.D. and Clive will be here tonight and will stay at the ranch.”

“All right, it’s decided,” Heath said. “We bring the women up to date at dinner tonight. Eric, you and Kade talk to Dana. Try to get her to leave but offer the cabin. The one next to Mitch is available. If she stays, Mitch, we’ll look to you to help her if things blow up.”

Mitch muttered a curse but nodded.

"We keep normal schedules as much as possible. The goal is to draw them to me." Kade glanced around the table. "Questions?"

Chapter Eighteen

"Come on, Dana, I'll introduce you to everyone." Amber took her by the arm, entering the great room to find people huddled up in small groups, talking. Annie saw them and moved to greet them.

"This must be Dana. I'm Annie MacLaren. Soon to be Amber's mother-in-law."

"I've heard a lot about you, Mrs. MacLaren."

"Call me Annie. Let's get you a drink then introduce you to the others." Annie took Dana's elbow, leaving Amber to find Eric.

Mitch spotted Dana right off, his irritation at having another woman to watch over hadn't lessened. In his mind, they should ship her home, get her out of danger, and spare themselves one more person to guard. Besides, she was a spit of a thing. Probably had no idea how to handle herself in a tough situation.

"And this is Cam and Mitch," Annie said. "Boys, this is Dana Ballard, Amber's friend. If you don't mind, I'll leave you three for a minute while I check on supper."

Cam extended his hand. "Dana, it's nice to meet you. Let me grab my wife, Lainey, and introduce you."

Dana watched him leave, then turned toward Mitch.

"So big guy, are you part of this tribe?" Dana smiled up at him, impressed in every way. She'd noticed him the moment she'd entered the room. Tall, muscled, with overlong hair, and what appeared to be a semi-permanent scowl on his face.

Mitch had never met anyone quite like Dana. Deep red hair framed a face sprinkled with freckles, and her bright blue eyes seemed to see everything as they darted around the room, then focused back on him. The intensity of her stare almost had him backing away.

"Tribe?"

"All right. Are you a Sinclair or MacLaren?"

Mitch groaned. Nothing he hated more than small talk. Especially with a female he didn't care to get to know. "MacLaren."

"I met Cassie already. You must be her brother."

"Cousin." He focused on his beer, trying to find a way to pass her off to someone else.

"Oh. The one from Montana. The surly one."

"Excuse me?"

"Not my words, of course."

Mitch groaned. "How long are you staying?" He had no problem with being called surly—it fit him just fine.

She laughed. Not some simpering, giggly, girl laugh, but full-throated and genuine. "You are a straight one, that's for sure."

"I see you've met our cousin, Mitch. Time to introduce you to his half-brother, Kade." Eric rested a hand on the small of Dana's back. For some reason, the gesture bothered Mitch, but damn if he knew why.

He watched as Eric introduced her to Kade, then Lainey before guiding her toward Amber.

"All right. Everyone grab a seat. Dinner's ready." Annie set the last of the bowls on the table, threw her apron on the counter, and took a seat next to Heath.

Eric sat next to Amber on one side while Dana took a seat on the other side. The two immediately launched into a conversation as the food began to be passed around. Dana stabbed a small cut of steak, if you could call any rib eye small.

"Grab me one of those, would you?"

The rough-edged voice came from right beside her. She looked over to see Mitch had taken a seat on her other side.

"Guess you drew the short straw," she joked as he speared a large steak and set it on his plate.

"Yeah. Guess so." There'd been other empty seats when he got to the table, but next to her was the closest, at least that's what he told himself.

The room drew silent, the clicking of silverware on plates the only noise.

Something had changed, Amber thought, as she looked around at the faces of the men. She'd first noticed it when returning from lunch with Dana. The mood around the office had grown tense and she wondered if the meeting Eric attended had anything to do with it.

Kade saw Heath nod at him, indicating the time had come to get down to business. He stood and tossed his napkin on the table. "We've got news." Kade went over what the men had decided during their meeting, ending by asking for questions. He answered a few then glanced at Dana.

"Dana, would you mind talking with Kade and me for a minute?" Eric asked. "You too, Amber."

Mitch watched Dana and Amber follow Eric and Kade toward Heath's study, and stood, deciding he wanted to listen in. After all, Heath had put him in charge of Dana, assuming she decided to stay, which in his opinion would make her a colossal fool. He strode in behind Kade, closed the door, and rested his back against it, crossing his arms.

"I know this is a surprise to you, Dana, and you need to know you don't have to stay," Eric said. "In fact, it would probably be best for you to pack up and head home to Denver. None of us have any idea how all this will play out and there's no sense in putting yourself in danger." Eric sat across from her in one of the large leather chairs, leaning forward and resting his arms on his legs, wishing all the women would leave the area.

Amber touched her friend's arm at the wounded look on Dana's face.

"He didn't mean it quite like it sounded." She shot Eric a stern look. "The truth is, no one wants you to get hurt because of something you walked into. We're all concerned for your safety. The decision, though, is up to you."

Dana glanced around the room, trying to decide what to do. "Just so I'm clear, Kade used to ride with a motorcycle gang and now these guys are after him?" Dana looked at Amber then back at Kade.

"That's the basics, yes. I was an undercover agent with the DEA when I was a member of Satan's Brethren Motorcycle Club. We took down their leader. That's why they're after me."

"I'm not sure how, but I've heard of them." She sat back, blew out a stream of air, and looked at Amber. "Quite a family you've hooked up with." Her light tone belied her concern for Amber more than fear for herself. "Of course, it's my own fault for driving out unannounced. If I stay, will I be at Amber's apartment?" she asked Eric.

"No. You'll be provided a cabin on the ranch. It's just a mile or so from my place, close to where Mitch is living. If you don't leave, it'll be the safest place for you."

"And it's for certain they're after you?" Dana asked Kade.

"As certain as it can be. Of course, we may be chasing something that isn't there. We won't know until it happens."

She thought it over for a moment, then let out a long breath. "The truth is, I've got nothing in Denver. I already gave notice on my apartment, put my furniture in storage, and I don't have a job. I might as well stay." Dana stood and walked over to a table where Heath kept his whisky. "This available for anyone?" She picked up a decanter full of golden colored liquid.

Eric nodded his head and stood. "Be our guest."

She grabbed a glass, filled it, and downed the contents in one swallow. "Okay. Someone show me this cabin where I'll be staying."

******

"This is it." Mitch pushed open the door to Dana's cabin, flipping on the porch light.

He'd followed her to Amber's apartment, waited while she grabbed her clothes, then drove back to the ranch. They made a brief stop at a convenience store for milk, bread, cereal, and fruit. As they turned onto a rutted dirt road, Mitch watched the old Jeep she drove bounce up and down behind him. It looked pretty beat up, but the engine sounded solid.

She looked around, surprised how large and airy it seemed. Mitch told her each cabin had two bedrooms and one bath, yet she still wasn't prepared for the comfy feel or beautiful view toward Fire Mountain. She turned in a circle, then faced Mitch.

"This is fabulous. Is yours like it?" She headed toward the kitchen, peeking in cupboards, and opening the refrigerator.

"An exact duplicate. It's the one we passed before pulling into your place."

She liked the sound of it—*her place.* Perhaps someday she would have a home as nice as this one. First she needed to find a regular job and wondered if the MacLarens would allow her to pay rent until then. She decided to speak with Amber about it.

"That makes us neighbors." She tossed him a saucy smile as she walked into the hall and stopped at the first doorway. "This is unbelievable. I can't believe they're letting me stay here." The bedroom contained a queen bed set in a pine frame, a pine dresser, desk, and chair.

Mitch walked up beside her, intrigued by her enthusiasm. It didn't seem like anything special to him, just a clean, furnished cabin for short-term use.

"Yeah...well, I guess I'll be going."

Dana followed him, then tapped his arm as he opened the door. "What is it you do for the company?"

His eyes narrowed on hers. He didn't have time for an inquisitive woman, not even one as pretty as Dana. "Whatever they need."

She watched as he turned his back to her and disappeared outside.

******

"Come in, gentlemen. We're glad you're here." Heath shook hands with DEA Special Agents J.D. Montalban and Clive Nelson. All family members who worked for the company were already in the room. "Good to see you again, Agent Nelson."

"Same here. Just wish it were under different circumstances."

Heath introduced them to the others, both agents nodding at Kade, who they'd met with late the night before. Unlike Clive's last trip when he stayed at the ranch, the two agents would be in a motel not far from the ranch entrance.

"If you don't mind, I'll go ahead and bring everyone up to date. Before I start, I want to stress that we believe no one is in immediate danger. If what we suspect is true, nothing will happen until Robbie Morgan arrives. And so we're clear, we don't have complete

230

confirmation Kade is a target. All of it is based on input from various third-party sources."

"But you believe it's accurate enough to bring you here," Eric said.

"True. As a precaution, we are here acting in unison with Sheriff Andrews and Chief Towers." Clive glanced at his notes. "We understand Kade has provided each of you with basic self-defense training. It's to be used to protect yourself. There are three groups of law enforcement participating in locating and capturing the men suspected of planning an attack on Kade—the sheriff and his deputies, the police chief and his officers, plus Agent Montalban and I." Clive passed out envelopes to each person. "The information in the packets is to be used for identification purposes and to let you know where the various law enforcement groups will be located. Contact information is included. Do not hesitate to reach out to us if you see anyone matching the descriptions of the club members."

Clive continued to explain what they could expect, reiterating more than once his concern for those in the club's path. "Being proactive, I would urge everyone except Kade to leave the area. If the club cannot find an easy way to pick up Kade, they will go after family. If you aren't here, you cannot be used against him."

"That's not going to happen, Clive, so what are the alternatives?" Eric asked, seeing the nods of agreement around the room.

"My gut told me that would be your response, Eric." Clive, the MacLarens, and Sinclairs had formed a bond the previous summer during another situation involving Kade and Brooke. He knew them to be a hands-on family when anyone needed their help. He also knew they had no intention of closing down business operations. "I believe Kade has gone over this before, but this is how we'll handle getting people to and from work, or other required destinations."

An hour later, Heath adjourned the meeting. "Eric, Kade, and Mitch, do you mind waiting behind a moment?" He shut the door, then took a seat next to Jace. "Blake is flying back to college tomorrow morning. Caroline and Annie are taking him to the airport and we've *encouraged* them to stay in the valley several extra days. Neither is happy about it, and they may just come home, but my hope is they'll stay until this situation blows over." He glanced at Jace, knowing the ire they'd caused with their request. "Cam, Lainey, and Cassie are flying to Cold Creek tomorrow afternoon. I've asked Cam to stay in Colorado until Morgan is in custody."

"I can imagine Cam's response." Eric leaned back in his seat and crossed his arms.

"It wasn't pretty," Heath replied. "That leaves us with Brooke, Amber, and Dana. Kade will keep track of Brooke. Eric, you're to keep tabs on Amber, and Mitch, we're asking you to keep watch on Dana."

Mitch leaned forward, resting his arms on the table. "My time would be better spent watching Kade's back than babysitting Dana."

"Perhaps, but Montalban and Nelson will have his back. If the club is watching the ranch, they know Dana is staying here. Therefore, she could be a target. We need someone to make sure she doesn't do anything—"

"Stupid," Mitch supplied. "We should've sent her away. She doesn't belong here."

"Maybe not, but she's here and you've got her." Heath watched Mitch's face move from irritation to acceptance. Rafe's oldest son was so much like him it was as if Heath were talking to his own brother and not his nephew. He turned his attention to the others. "I want everyone to work from home as much as possible. No sense leaving the ranch unless it's required.

"Keith Vance and an associate are flying in Thursday morning from San Antonio for our meeting," Eric reminded them. "Amber will take them to lunch then bring them to the conference room for their presentation. They fly out afterwards, so no dinner plans.”

“Who’s scheduled to attend?” Jace asked.

“Everyone in this room plus Amber and Brooke.”

“Brooke will be riding with Eric and Amber. I don’t want her in the car with me.” Kade wasn’t keen on his role of keeping track of Brooke. He needed to be a target for Robbie and wanted his wife as far away from him as possible. He’d speak to Heath after the meeting.

“All right. Any other meetings that can’t be rescheduled?” Jace asked.

When no one responded, Heath stood. “That’s it.”

Kade stayed behind as the others left.

“What’s on your mind?” Heath asked.

“I want you to keep watch on Brooke. The plan is for me to be visible. We want Robbie and his boys to come after me and no one else. In fact, I’d prefer she stay at your place.”

“Has she agreed to that?”

“Hell no.” Kade ran a hand through his hair. “At least I can drop her at your place each morning. Will that work?”

“Or at my place if Heath has to leave. Between the two of us, we can keep track of her.

You do what you have to do, Kade." Jace glanced at his watch. "I have to take off. Promised Blake I'd spend time with him before he left."

Kade turned to follow Jace out.

"Kade?"

He turned back toward Heath.

"The family knows you had a job to do with the DEA, and you did it. No one faults you or believes you brought this down on us. Sonny Morgan and his club are the bad guys here." He walked over and clasped a hand on his nephew's shoulder. "Don't take any unnecessary risks. We don't intend to lose you."

Kade met Heath's gaze and nodded, swallowing the lump in his throat, and hoping all would turn out all right.

******

"How's your schedule?" Eric asked as he walked into Amber's office and shut the door.

"Five more minutes and I'm done." She took a couple of steps and put her arms around his neck, reaching up to place a kiss on his mouth. "You have something in mind?" She wiggled her brows slightly.

"You're insatiable." Eric laughed and wrapped his arms around her waist, pulling her close.

"You wouldn't have it any other way."

"You're right about that." He lowered his mouth to hers, knowing it wasn't the smartest move to get anything going in the office. Just a couple of kisses and he'd pull away.

Amber felt the slide of his tongue against hers, the slight taste of coffee on his lips, and the warmth of his body. She knew how quickly she could get lost in the feel of him and pulled back to rest her head against his chest.

"This probably isn't wise." Her thick voice indicated how fast his touch affected her.

"What's Dana doing tonight?"

Her mouth tipped up at the corners. "She asked if it would be okay if she grabbed something by herself so she could prepare for an interview tomorrow morning."

"No kidding?"

"Uh...uh." She placed a kiss on his chin then moved her lips along his jaw.

He reached for her hand. "Grab your stuff and let's get out of here. I know a little cabin a few miles away with a fully stocked refrigerator..." his words trailed off as he led her outside to the parking lot.

Chapter Nineteen

"Anything I can carry out?" Eric asked, stepping into Jace and Caroline's house. He and Amber decided to stop on their way to the office Wednesday morning and say goodbye to Blake.

"Nope. I'm all packed." Blake shoved his hands in his pockets, his voice flat.

"You okay?" Eric searched his face, seeing none of the positive attitude everyone associated with the young man. "Are you sure you're recovered enough to travel?"

"It's not that. I just don't want to leave with everything going on." Blake looked up at Eric. "You know, with Kade."

He wrapped an arm around Blake's shoulder and moved them a few feet away. "My hunch is you leaving is the only way Jace and Heath can get your mother and Annie out of here. They refused to leave."

Blake looked over his shoulder at his mother and aunt. "You think so?"

"Heath and Jace were frantic to get them to leave. I don't know what leverage they used to get them to stay at the condo afterwards, but you're the mechanism to get them to the valley." He let his arm drop. "I need to talk with my mom before you leave." Eric walked over to Annie, giving her a hug and kiss. "I hear you're staying in the valley a while."

He could see Annie's face tighten. "I won't go into details, but it's not my choice—or Caroline's."

"Should I ask?"

"No." She crossed her arms, a sure sign the topic had ended.

"Do you need me to load anything?" He glanced across the room to Amber helping Caroline with a small bag.

"I'm set and I think Caroline is about ready."

They walked to the large SUV Caroline drove.

"Call us when you get there." Eric closed the passenger door for his mother and stepped back.

Annie rolled down her window and leaned out, her concern obvious. "You be safe."

"We will, Mom."

Amber and Eric waved as the SUV headed toward the highway.

"I'm glad they're getting out of here." He turned to face her. "I wish you, Brooke, and Dana would leave, too."

"I won't leave unless you do, and I know Brooke feels the same way about Kade." She squeezed his hand. "Guess you're stuck with us."

******

"You'll need to fly out this afternoon with Lainey and me on the company jet. Will that be an issue?" Cam asked Cassie as they sat in his office Wednesday morning, reviewing the organization chart for the Cold Creek, Colorado facility. MacLaren Bucking Broncs had grown substantially under Cam's leadership, and his plans were to double the revenue over the next year.

"Not at all, except I hate to leave with the threat hanging over Kade."

"So do I, but we can't shut down while we wait. We may not get back here for a week or two. You can stay with us—there's plenty of room." Cam hid his irritation at being told he, Lainey, and Cassie would be leaving for Colorado. He'd put up a strong argument, but in the end, Heath and Jace had made up their

239

minds to do all they could to limit any possible danger.

Cassie had trained under Cam and Jace at company headquarters since graduating from college. For years her goal had been to work with the horses they bred for the rodeo circuit, and now her chance had arrived. She grew up on the ranch, trained horses for pleasure riding, and gave lessons every summer. The time had come to branch out and learn the business of supplying stock to the hundreds of rodeos across the country—a competitive business run almost exclusively by men. Many of their competitors hired ex-rodeo contestants with existing connections that opened doors.

Cassie read over the job description and travel schedule. She'd be working under Sonny Burrows, the head of rodeo relations, traveling the circuit, and meeting with his long list of contacts. Everyone knew Sonny, respected him, but he'd indicated a need to slow down. Cassie hoped she'd be good enough to take his place when he decided to retire.

"Sonny's travel schedule is crazy." She glanced up at Cam. "No wonder he's ready to bring on an assistant."

"I won't kid you. He isn't keen on a woman tailing him for months while he works. The fact you're a MacLaren is one plus in a long list of negatives." Cam chuckled, remembering the look on Sonny's face when he handed him Cassie's résumé. "He's old school."

"But teachable?" she joked.

"In my opinion, yes. He's a good man, works hard, and relishes the challenge of going up against the new upstarts trying to capture business it took him years to earn." Cam's eyes narrowed on her. "It's a hard, tough business. You need to be prepared to deal with the unscrupulous as well as those with principles. You may face corruption and bribery. What some call *back room deals* are common. Sonny will tell you these private negotiations are the key to winning rodeo contracts, and in the same breath, warn that you might never break into them. You've got to be in this for the long term, Cassie."

She grew up surrounded by men and the male friendships that made business happen. Her short stint in the amateur barrel racing circuit added to her understanding of rodeo operations. It's why she'd earned a business degree, graduating near the top of her class. Nothing had prepared her for the situations Cam described.

"Working in the family business is what I've wanted since before high school. With the expansions, and pulling Rafe back into the family, I can't imagine working anywhere else." She worried her lower lip, then sat up straight, fixing her gaze on Cam. "I can do this job. I'll go to Sonny, or you, if I see anything I'm not sure about—but I won't back down or walk away."

Cam leaned back in his chair, glanced at his watch, and smiled. "Never thought you would. Go get packed. We'll meet you at the air field in three hours."

$$******$$

Dana walked into the restaurant and straight to the table where Amber and Eric sat, sipping their drinks. She'd applied everywhere in town for any position related to graphic design, expecting it could take weeks to land a job.

"Hey. You look pleased with yourself," Amber said as Dana took a seat.

"You won't guess what happened."

Amber glanced at Eric, then shrugged, knowing by her friend's broad smile the news would be good.

"I've been hired by the community college to take over two graphic design classes another instructor had to give up." She reached across the table to high-five Amber. "I start next week, and if all goes well, they may keep me through the rest of the year and possibly longer." She took a long swallow of the soda their waitress set down, then grabbed a menu. "I'll still need other work, but it's a start."

"Two classes?" Eric asked, knowing Amber would be thrilled to have Dana close by in Fire Mountain.

"Yep. Both are for beginning designers. One on theory and the other on technique. They gave me the previous instructor's syllabus." She took a deep breath. "I still can't believe it."

"We need to celebrate. How about dinner tonight with us, Kade and Brooke, and Mitch at the Italian place everyone likes?" Amber squeezed Eric's hand, hoping everyone could attend.

"I'm not sure it's that big a deal. I don't want to mess up anyone's plans." She didn't want to make more of it than it was, and she didn't need to spend an evening with Mitch and his sour outlook.

"Not a problem. Brooke and I already talked about it. Now we have a reason to party. And right now, any reason is good."

******

"Hop in. We'll swing by to get Dana, then head to the restaurant." Eric rolled up his window, not seeing the irritation on Mitch's face.

Mitch slid into the back seat of Eric's truck.

Amber turned to look at Mitch, sensing something about Dana didn't set well with him. "Thanks for helping her move into the cabin. I know she appreciated it."

"All I did was haul a couple of bags in. Nothing more." He crossed his arms and sat back, pushing his hat down low over his brow.

"Do you mind getting her, Mitch?" Eric pulled to a stop.

He didn't respond, just climbed out and walked up to Dana's door, which pulled open before he could knock. "Guess you're ready."

"Starving is more like it. Amber says the food is great." She didn't wait to see if he'd follow her as she walked around to the passenger side behind Amber. She climbed in before Mitch could catch up with her to open the door.

Eric stopped at Kade and Brooke's cabin last, seeing them come out the front door. "It'll be tight, but there's no reason to take two cars."

Kade opened Amber's door and helped Brooke up, then climbed in beside Dana in the back.

The last person Dana wanted to be this close to groaned as her thigh touched his. "Sorry. It will only be for a little while." *I hope*, she thought and clasped her hands in her lap.

The ride took less than twenty minutes, but to Mitch it felt like an eternity. He didn't like the woman beside him. She was too pushy, too mouthy, and over the top in about everything she did. He liked women who knew how to be quiet, enjoyed simple pleasures, and didn't ask a lot of questions.

"Amber mentioned Cam, Lainey, and Cassie left for Cold Creek this afternoon. Do you have plans to take off, also?" Dana glanced at Mitch, waiting.

"Nope."

"I've been to Cold Creek a few times. Beautiful area on the western slope. Have you been there?"

"Yep."

Dana heard Kade snicker and decided to take the hint, believing the description of Mitch as surly fit him well. She'd been in Fire Mountain less than a week and already felt good about everyone in Amber's soon-to-be family, except for Mitch. His brusque manner was at odds with the rest of the MacLarens and Sinclairs.

Amber's description of the restaurant fit. Warm reds and subdued orange hues covered the walls, which held a selection of old west images framed in dark woods. Flames blazed in the rock fireplace and the soft lighting felt welcoming. The hostess escorted them to a table in the middle.

"How's your family, Eric?" The waitress, about his age, offered a broad smile to the group.

"All's good. How about yours?"

"Same 'ole, same 'ole. Dad works too hard in the restaurant and mom won't rest unless he does. So they both wear themselves out." She shook her head. "It never changes. So, what can I get everyone?"

It took little time for the food to be placed before them—big, heaping portions, which covered their plates.

"This smells wonderful." Dana leaned down to breathe in the aroma of her chicken marsala. "What did you get, Mitch?"

He glanced over at her, just inches away. "Spaghetti and meatballs."

"Really? With all the great choices, you opted for spaghetti?"

"With meatballs."

The others glanced at each other, concealing their amusement. Few people pushed Mitch and it was good to see Dana punch his buttons. Eric picked up his glass of wine.

"To good friends and family." The others joined in the toast, then dug in, the table quieting except for moans of approval.

Kade finished first and pushed away his plate. "Man, that was great." He reached out to pick up his wine glass when his phone rang. "Taylor." He stood, walking toward the entrance, then stepped outside.

The others tensed, wondering if the call had to do with Robbie Morgan. They didn't need to wonder for long. Kade walked back inside, his face a mask.

"They lost Morgan and his boys somewhere outside of Albuquerque."

Brooke shot a look at Eric then looked back at Kade. "What does that mean?"

"Means we have no idea where the S.O.B. is. Sorry ladies." He scrubbed a hand over his face and grabbed his wine, emptying the glass. "Clive thinks they traded bikes with brothers in the Albuquerque chapter, packed their colors, and are taking a different route. He and J.D. are still convinced they're coming this way. He's already been in touch with Sheriff Andrews and Chief Towers." He reached out and grabbed Brooke's hand. "I have to meet with Clive and J.D. tonight."

"I'm going with you," Eric said and narrowed his gaze on Kade. "Don't try to talk me out of it."

"Me, too," Mitch said and stood. "Let's get out of here."

******

"Where are you?" Swinger walked outside the house that felt like a prison after three weeks and held the phone to his ear.

"Four Corners. We'll stay here tonight, maybe longer." Robbie and his boys found rooms in an old motel at the junction of Colorado, New Mexico, Arizona, and Utah. The owner was well-known to bikers, keeping quiet about the identities of those who stayed at his place. "We'll stay here until I'm certain no one is following us."

"You think the feds are watching?"

"We haven't seen anyone. Just being cautious." Robbie glanced around at the almost deserted lot. The old biker said he had only one other group of riders staying tonight. "We swapped bikes in Albuquerque. What's happening there?"

"Taylor's here. He's going about his business like he has no idea he's a target."

"Don't underestimate him. Look how he fooled us, and Sonny—which is damn hard to do. I'll guarantee he fuckin' well knows we'll come after him."

"He's out tonight with his old lady and others who live on the ranch. Joker and one of the boys are watching him. We bought an old pickup truck. Paid cash. I gotta tell you, Robbie, I'm thinkin' more about going after his old lady."

"We'll decide when I get there." Robbie hung up and shoved the phone in his pocket. He didn't like the idea of going after a woman, but Taylor had put her in danger, not Robbie. The man knew the risks of fuckin' with Satan's Brethren, which included painting a target on his family. They'd do whatever was necessary to bring down the ex-brother who'd betrayed them

and arrested Sonny—and his death would not be
an easy one.

Chapter Twenty

"You must be Miss Anderson. I'm Kevin Vance, and this is my associate, Jax Perry. I appreciate you meeting us for lunch."

"It's a pleasure to meet you both." Amber shook their hands, "I called ahead for reservations."

Kevin pulled the entry door open and stepped aside as the women walked past him, then followed the hostess to a booth near a window. "Nice place."

"It's convenient, the food is good, and it's quiet." Amber opened her menu, eyeing Jax over the top of it, trying to conceal her curiosity about the woman.

"Have you worked for MacLaren long?" Jax asked Amber after they'd ordered.

"Almost two months."

"And what do you do for them?"

"I'm in charge of marketing for all their groups. I know Kevin has been working with Eric. Have you also worked with him?" She glanced at Jax, wondering about her affiliation with Eric.

Jax glanced at Kevin before flashing Amber a too sweet smile. "I wouldn't call it work, exactly." She took a sip of her water. "I suppose you could say I know him socially."

"Ah...I see."

"Yes. We became quite good friends after Kevin introduced us."

Seeing the look of surprise on Amber's face, Kevin glanced at Jax, annoyance clear in his expression. "Jax handles much of the marketing for our clients. I introduced Eric and Jax when we first began to work together. I thought perhaps she could provide her insights on marketing in the San Antonio area."

"How thoughtful of you. I'm certain Jax and I can learn a lot from each other."

Amber's stomach clenched as she tried to make sense of Jax's relationship with Eric. She knew the association with Kevin had begun shortly before Amber started at MacLaren. Eric had made a couple of trips to San Antonio since, one just before they'd become engaged less than a week before. He hadn't left town since. Still, Amber wondered if she knew Eric as well as she thought. Maybe he had changed. She'd known other men, both in New York and Denver, who appeared happily married, then learned they thought nothing of keeping another woman on the side.

"Your presentation is set for two o'clock. If there's time before then, perhaps you and I can sit down for a few minutes to discuss your thoughts on the San Antonio market." Amber finished what she could of her lunch, leaving over half untouched on the plate.

They walked into MacLaren headquarters at one thirty, Amber turning to Kevin and Jax.

"Let me see if Eric's back from his lunch appointment." She left them in a waiting area outside the executive offices and tapped on Eric's door before opening it. He sat at his desk, the phone to his ear, and reached an arm out to her, encouraging Amber to come up beside him. She shook her head, not moving from her place on the other side of his desk.

He eyed her, wondering at the disturbed look. He hung up and sat forward, his brows knitting together.

"Kevin is here, along with his associate—Jax Perry."

Eric's expression hardened as he began to understand her odd behavior.

"Jax gave the impression the two of you are quite good friends."

He stood, making no attempt to walk toward her and took a deep breath. "Let me explain—"

"When did you last see her?"

"Two weeks ago when I was in San Antonio." He eyed her, not liking the wariness he saw. "She was coming out of a meeting with Kevin, then she left."

"Did you ever sleep with her?"

"Yes." He walked around the desk, needing to get closer to her. She backed up, creating more distance. "One time. Before you came to work here. I haven't been with her since."

"I see."

"No, I don't think you do. Jax and I were together once. One. Time. Only. There's been no one since you showed up, Amber." He tried again to step toward her, but she walked toward the door and pulled it open.

"They're in the waiting area."

He glanced at her left hand, noting she still wore his engagement ring. "I love you, Amber. Jax and I were a one-time thing—nothing more."

She swallowed the lump in her throat, needing to believe him, and nodded. "I understand."

He followed her down the hall, extending a hand to Kevin.

"It's good to see you, Eric. You know Jax, of course."

"Hello, Jax. I didn't know you were the associate Kevin mentioned would be joining us."

She walked up to him, ignoring his hand, and gave him a brief hug while placing a kiss on his cheek. "It's good to see you. When Kevin mentioned traveling to Fire Mountain, I told him I wanted to come along."

He backed away and looked at Amber. "I understand you've met my fiancée, Amber Anderson."

Jax's eyes widened at the news.

Kevin stepped forward, hiding his shock. "She didn't mention your engagement to us. Congratulations, Eric. I'm sure you'll be very happy."

Eric shot a look at Jax. "I know we will. Let me show you to the conference room where you can set up while I get the others."

******

"Thanks for taking the time to meet with us, Kevin. I'll get together with the rest of the management team to review your suggestions, then have Eric get in touch."

"I'm glad you found the information useful. Let me know if you have any questions." He watched Heath leave, followed by everyone except Eric. Kevin packed up his folders before turning to Jax. "Looks like we have plenty of time to make our flight."

"I'd like to have a few words with Eric."

Kevin nodded, still showing the irritation which had been simmering since the lunch with Amber. He'd never seen Jax behave with less than the upmost professionalism and regretted his decision to bring her along. He walked out, leaving the two alone.

"My understanding when we met was that you had no one in your life. I wish I'd known about her."

Eric didn't blame the accusation in her voice. "When you and I got together, I had no attachments, Jax, and no plans to develop a relationship with anyone. Amber and I weren't together then."

"If I'd known, I never would have come here."

Eric shoved his hands in his pockets. "It didn't occur to me to mention Amber when I saw you at Kevin's office during my last trip to San Antonio. I won't go into details, but I've known Amber since high school. I hadn't seen her in years, not until Heath introduced her as our new marketing director, which was after I'd met you. The relationship moved rather quickly from there."

"She must be quite special."

"She is." Eric glanced at the door, wanting to find Amber and make sure everything was all right. "I've been in love with her a long time."

Jax heard the sincerity in his voice. "I truly do wish you the best, Eric, and hope this won't impact your business with Kevin. He's a good man, and I know he'll do a great job for MacLaren." She left without another word.

******

Eric stood outside Amber's office door, hearing her speaking on the phone, waiting to knock. If their engagement hadn't been so new, he might not feel the apprehension at her reaction to Jax, a woman he liked, but nothing more. He heard her hang up and knocked.

"Yes?"

He walked in and closed the door behind him, leaning his back against it, and crossing his arms. He stared at her a moment, trying to gauge her mood. "Are you okay?"

Amber moved around her desk to lean against it, her hands grabbing the edges on either side of her.

"She's quite beautiful. I can see why you'd be attracted to her."

"Yes, she is beautiful." He dropped his arms to his sides and pushed away from the door. "The problem is, she isn't you. I know things have moved fast between us and there are a lot we still need to talk about, but trust me when I tell you that you're who I want. No one else."

Amber never saw herself as a woman possessed of much drama. She had no intention of making this more than what it was or blowing it up to create a wedge between her and Eric. However, the warning signals in her head cautioned her to slow the pace, make certain they were making the right decision to marry.

"So much has happened since I arrived, including dealing with the danger to your family. I wonder if we're rushing this." She held up her left hand, indicating the engagement ring. "Do you think we're moving too fast?"

"No. If there's anything I regret, it's not hunting you down sooner. I never should've let you leave California when every instinct I had told me to stop you, force us to talk it through. Pride got in my way." He moved up to within inches of her. "I won't let anything come between us this time."

"We both have pasts the other knows nothing about." Her whispered voice shook as Eric let his knuckles slide down her cheek.

"If it's important to you, we'll fill in the gaps."

"It's not important to you?" Her voice quivered as his hand moved down her arm and grasped her hand.

"No, but it's not that I have no interest in learning what's happened in your life since we split up. I just don't need to know the details of the relationships you've had. I want to move forward, just you and me, forgetting about the mistakes we've made. Can we do that?"

She looked at their joined hands, then gazed up at his face, offering a tentative smile. "Yes, I believe we can."

He pulled her to him, letting out a breath he hadn't realized he'd been holding. His hands moved up her back, rubbing small circles as he rested his chin on the top of her head, feeling her relax against him.

She laid her head against his chest, hearing his heartbeat, and feeling the warmth of his body pass to hers. He'd had other women since their split, lots of them from what she'd learned, but none of them mattered. He was hers again, and she'd hold on to her last breath to keep him.

******

"All I need is a ride from the auto shop to the cabin. I wouldn't be calling you if I'd been able to reach Amber or Eric." Dana let out a frustrated breath. The last person she'd wanted to call offered a mumbled oath into the phone.

"Fine. Stay where you are and I'll pick you up in thirty minutes." Mitch hung up. He'd just arrived at his place, making the decision to take his motorcycle out for a quick ride before settling in for a night of reviewing contracts for the MacLaren bucking bull operations in Montana. Someday his father, Rafe, expected him to take over the presidency from him. To do that, he needed to learn not just about the bull business but also the other operations in the MacLaren empire.

He set his helmet back on the shelf, intending to take his truck, then changed his mind and grabbed two helmets. If she needed his help, she'd just have to settle for what he offered.

Dana watched as one set of headlights after another sped past the auto shop. She'd worn a skirt for the interview a few blocks away. By Monday she hoped to hear if she'd won the part-time job as a graphic designer for a fledgling advertising firm. The teaching position plus this one would be what she needed to sustain herself until she found a more permanent job.

She heard the rumble of a motorcycle and looked up to see it slow before pulling into the parking area, stopping a few feet from her. Dana ignored it, scanning the cars moving past, hoping he'd arrive soon.

"Well, you going to get on or not?"

She swung her gaze to the rider who removed his helmet. Mitch glared at her, an impatient gleam in his eyes. She checked her watch. Thirty minutes exactly. At least he could tell time. She straightened her skirt and walked up to him.

"Nice ride. Is this my helmet?" She pointed to one secured at the back.

He nodded, her reaction not what he'd hoped. Mitch thought she'd back away, run inside, and call a cab. Instead, her appreciative gaze wandered over the bike, noticing the details most people ignored.

"Do you want to hop on the back?" she asked, amusement clear on her face.

"Hell no." He nodded for her to get on behind him.

Dana lifted her skirt and slipped her right leg behind him, then settled into the backseat, wrapping her arms around his waist. "Let's go, Galahad."

What had he expected? Mitch asked himself as they made their way through evening traffic. The woman continued to surprise him. Nothing seemed to phase her, not even his beast of a Harley, or riding behind him in a skirt that rode up to her hips. He spotted a burger place he liked and pulled in, riding up to the order window, and looking over his shoulder at Dana.

"What do you want?"

"Double cheese burger, double fries, and a chocolate shake. Oh, and one of those berry turnover things they have."

Mitch shook his head. That was more than most of his friends ate. He doubled the order and pulled up to the next window as the noise of several motorcycles came up from behind them. He shifted in the seat to look over his right shoulder. Six bikes entered the lot. A couple pulled a few feet away, others crowded behind him at the pickup window, and two stopped just shy of blocking the exit. One, who Mitch suspected of being the leader, stopped so his handlebars touched Mitch's and stared at him while keeping his bike running.

Dana leaned forward to within an inch of his ear. "Ignore them."

"No shit," he answered as he paid for the food and handed the bags to Dana. "Hold on. We're out of here."

Mitch pulled into a break in traffic, gunning the bike, and moving past the cars ahead of him until he'd put a comfortable distance between them and the bikers. Fifteen minutes later they stopped in front of Dana's cabin. He got off and grabbed the bags of food, then followed her into the house.

She opened her purse, rummaged for money, then handed him what she thought her food cost.

"Forget it. Save your money to pay for that wreck of a Jeep of yours." He set the food on the kitchen counter and dug inside until he pulled out two burgers, handing one to Dana.

"She works great. Just had a little hiccup today." She grabbed the burger from his hand, unwrapped it, and bit off a large bite. "I'll pit her against that truck of yours any day."

Mitch almost choked on his food. "You're on."

"Can I take her out someday?"

"Who?" he asked, taking a gulp of his soda.

"Your bagger. Can I ride her sometime?"

Mitch set down his soda and cocked his head. "You're talking about my bike?"

She nodded, concentrating on her food.

"No one rides my bike. Especially not some inexperienced squirt of a thing like you."

Her eyes widened then narrowed on him. She had become used to this reaction from male bikers. "I'll bet you let Eric and Kade take her out."

"Sure. They're my brothers. You? You're..." he didn't know what to say as she stood a foot away, glaring at him.

"I can handle her as well as anyone."

"Well, I guess we aren't going to find out." He finished his second burger, popped the last fry in his mouth, and crumbled the bag before heading toward the door, then stopped to pull out his phone. He dialed Kade's number, getting voicemail.

"Call me. It's important." He hung up and dialed Eric. "It's Mitch. I saw a group of six riders at the burger place about an hour ago. Their colors read Devil's Sons. You ever heard of them?"

"No. Kade is at Heath's place. Where are you now?" Eric set the phone on speaker so Amber could hear.

"At Dana's."

"Oh, yeah?" Eric chuckled into the phone.

"I don't want any crap from you, Sinclair. She needed a ride—that's all. I'm heading to Heath's."

"I'll meet you there."

Mitch shoved his phone in his pocket then turned toward Dana. "Call Amber when you need a ride to pick up your Jeep." He stepped outside, pulled the door closed with a slam.

Jerk, Dana thought as she heard his bike start up and pull away. She dialed Amber.

"Hey, guess you got my voicemail about my car being in the shop. I'm not sure if it will be ready tomorrow or Monday."

"No problem. We can scrounge up a car for you to use in the meantime, then I'll take you to pick up yours when it's ready." Amber peered through the blinds to see Eric leave. He'd promised to call if they learned anything about the riders Mitch had spotted. "Why don't I come over for a while?"

"Sounds good. Oh, I hope you've eaten because I have nothing." Dana opened the refrigerator to see a carton of milk, eggs, mayonnaise, mustard, a bottle of wine, and beer. "Unless you want egg sandwiches," she laughed.

"I'm good. I'll contact Brooke, too. See you in a few minutes."

Chapter Twenty-One

"Does anyone recognize the name?" Eric asked the group of men congregating in Heath's study. Clive and J.D. had arrived a few minutes before after a meeting with Sheriff Andrews.

"They're a support group to Satan's Brethren," Kade answered. "I was afraid this might happen."

"What?" Eric asked.

"At first I thought Robbie would keep the hunt for me within the Brethren. Looks like he decided the help of his support club, Devil's Sons, is worth the risk of being discovered. They're a bunch of wild cards with little allegiance to anyone—not even the Brethren."

"Riding up to Mitch seems pretty bold if Robbie wants to keep it quiet." Clive jotted down notes, then closed the binder.

"Intimidation, maybe." Eric didn't like the idea of the gang announcing their presence. "At least now we know the threat is real."

"Where are the women tonight?" Heath asked.

"Amber texted me that she and Brooke are at Dana's." Eric pulled out his phone confirming he'd received no other messages.

Heath pinched the bridge of his nose between his thumb and forefinger. "I want everyone to work from home tomorrow."

"What about travel?" Mitch asked.

"I've asked Cam to stay in Cold Creek with Lainey and Cassie. Rafe is staying in Montana, although reluctantly. We're asking for trouble riding back and forth between here, the office, and airport. Phyllis will reschedule meetings or travel. Let her know."

"And the weekend? Are we still planning to try and draw them out?" Eric, Mitch, and Kade had planned to ride out on Saturday in an attempt to draw the gang's attention.

"I'd suggest holding off on that until we have more information on Robbie's location. I'd recommend limiting your activities off the ranch. If you leave, go in groups of no less than three people and let Clive or I know where you're headed," J.D. said.

"Health's right. This is heating up fast and will escalate quickly when Robbie gets here. There's no point in thinking he won't show. The

Devil's Sons making themselves known in Fire Mountain leaves no doubt about what's going on. Frankly, everyone should plan to stay on the ranch until this is over." Clive nodded toward J.D. "We'll let you know if Robbie is spotted in the area."

******

"Why don't you ride to Dana's with us? Have a beer and relax." Eric suggested as Mitch climbed on his motorcycle. "No sense going back to an empty cabin."

"I'll pass." Mitch settled his helmet on his head then glanced at Kade. "Let me know if you hear anything." He gunned his engine and took off.

"Is he all right?" Kade asked as he pulled up next to Eric's truck.

"Damned if I know."

******

Swinger stood outside the rented house on Sunday morning, hands on hips, listening for the sound of motorcycles. Robbie called an hour before saying he and the others would be arriving and to be prepared to call church.

269

They'd had no need for the regular club meetings since Swinger and Joker left for Arizona. Church today would be their first meeting in weeks.

A few minutes later he heard the unmistakable rumble of bikes, followed by a cloud of dust where the riders hit the dirt road. Several bikes pulled into the large front yard. Robbie cut his engine, removed his half-shell beanie, and walked toward Swinger, gripping his brother's hand.

"Glad you're here." Swinger guided Robbie a few feet away, speaking in low tones. "The Devil's Sons are fuckin' around, ignoring orders, and pulling all kinds of shit."

"What about Javé?" Everyone used the man's shortened nickname, although the full name fit—Javelina—a short, ugly pig with a distinctive odor.

"Gone most of the time. It's bad, Robbie. I say we kick their butts out of here and do it with the brothers we trust."

Robbie nodded. He didn't need this kind of stuff going down during something this important. They'd have one chance at this and they didn't need screw-ups. "When's church?"

"As soon as you're ready."

"Grab me a beer and we'll do it now." He followed Swinger into the house, shook hands with Joker and the other members of Satan's Brethren, then positioned himself against a wall, looking at the six members of their support club. He took a long swallow of his beer then slammed the bottle on a nearby table, drawing everyone's attention.

"Where's Javé?" The hard edge to his voice left no doubt about his frustration. When no one answered, he asked again. "Someone had better tell me where Javé is or there'll be hell to pay."

"At Rosa's."

"Who are you?" Robbie asked, not recognizing him.

"Chef." He indicated the name patch on his cut.

"Chef?"

The kid shrugged. "Yeah. I like to cook."

Robbie cast a look at Swinger and grinned, maybe the first smile he'd allowed himself in weeks.

"Where's this Rosa woman, Chef?"

"He's got her at some motel up the highway. Told us to let him know when you got here."

"All of you." He pointed to the members of Devil's Sons seated across the room. "Follow Chef to where Javé is located. Stay there. Tell him I'll be in touch and not to leave until I give the word."

"Javé said we should wait here for him." A slender man with a stringy beard and big gut continued to sit, ignoring Robbie's order. Robbie took several long strides before reaching down and grabbing the man by the shirt, jerking him up.

"I won't ask nicely again, shithead. Get the hell out of here," he thundered. "I'll be in touch." Robbie shoved the man against a wall. "And I don't want to see any of you assholes around here unless I give the okay. You hear me?"

Swinger handed Robbie another beer as they waited for the gang to leave.

"They out of it?" Swinger asked.

"Unless there's no chance we can grab Taylor without them. I'll deal with Javé and his disrespect later." Robbie chugged down half his beer then took a seat at a nearby table. He pounded three times, ready to get their meeting started. "Church is in session."

******

"I'm going over a couple of current projects with Brooke, then I'll be ready to take you to the auto shop. How about I call you as soon as we're finished. Okay...sounds good." Amber hung up and checked her watch. Eleven o'clock on Monday morning.

The weekend had come and gone without additional sightings of the motorcycle gang Mitch had seen Thursday night. Eric, Amber, and Dana had driven to town once for groceries, returning with enough food for everyone at the ranch.

The previous night, she and Eric invited Dana and Mitch over for dinner. At first Mitch declined, then changed his mind when Eric mentioned there'd be steak and his favorite pie. Another night of his own cooking didn't hold much appeal compared to Amber's. The evening had gone as expected.

Dana asked Mitch a lot of questions about his motorcycle, where he rode, and tried to convince him to let her take it out for a ride—which he refused, even though Amber vouched for her friend's riding skills. Mitch tolerated her for the sake of peace and a large slice of berry pie. Neither Eric nor Amber understood what caused the tension between the two, guessing Dana's strong personality and sense of humor plus Mitch's churlish attitude meshed like oil and water.

Even though the last few days had been quiet, Heath insisted everyone stay put on Monday, and every day afterwards until the situation had been resolved. Today, Eric, Kade, Mitch, Heath, and Jace were working at the main house while Amber went over some marketing ideas with Brooke at Eric's cabin.

"Why don't I go with you? J.D. mentioned going in groups of three, and we could grab something to eat." Brooke had stared at the same walls for four days except for the three walks she took with Kade and a quick trip to the ranch house to make sure Heath and Jace were okay. "When we get back, maybe I can talk Heath into letting us take the horses out for a ride."

"Great idea. Let's finish this and pick up Dana."

******

An hour later, the three climbed into Brooke's red SUV and took the main drive past the ranch house and onto the highway. They'd been so caught up in conversation that none of them had thought to notify the men until they were a few miles from the ranch.

"Did you let Eric know we were leaving?" Brooke asked, turning toward the restaurant where they decided to have lunch. They'd pick up Dana's car afterward, making a short side trip to drop off some clothes at their favorite charity.

"I thought you called Kade. Guess I'd better let them know." She grabbed her phone just as it started to ring. "Hello."

"Where are you?" Eric's voice sounded strained and none too friendly.

"Brooke, Dana, and I are going to lunch then picking up Dana's car."

"What the hell were you thinking taking off without letting us know?" She could hear the anger in his voice and knew how worried he was, even though they'd been gone less than twenty minutes.

"You're right. We shouldn't have left without calling, but now we're here and have seen nothing. The road's been clear, no motorcycles, and no one's tailing us."

"And you know that how?"

"Well...I've seen how they do it on television. You know, checking behind us while Brooke drives. We're fine, Eric. How about I call you when we leave the restaurant to get Dana's Jeep?"

"I want to hear from you in an hour, no longer than that."

"All right. An hour. You'll let Kade know what's going on?" She glanced through the windshield. "Oh, we're here. I'll call you in a little bit." She hung up before Eric could respond. "He's not pleased, and that's being generous. He'll let Kade and the others know what's happening."

Amber called Eric back an hour later as they walked to Brooke's car. She could tell their trip had caused a lot of tension at the house, but there wasn't anything they could do about it now. They dropped off the clothes, then Brooke pulled onto the street, looking at Dana in the rearview mirror.

"Where is this place?" Brooke asked.

"Do you know the burger shop Mitch likes?"

"Yes."

"It's about a mile past that on the right. I'll show you when we get close." Dana checked her messages, seeing she'd missed a call from the advertising firm where she interviewed the previous week. She called back and left a message when no one picked up. "Up there on the right."

Brooke pulled to a stop in a gravel lot. Dana jumped out with Amber and Brooke following behind.

"Is Gus here?" she asked a young man in the office. He looked up, his eyes darting around as he licked his lips in a nervous gesture.

"Uh...no. He had to leave for a while. Can I help you?"

"I talked to him this morning. He said my Jeep's ready."

"The yellow one with a hard top?" He shifted papers around, not meeting her gaze.

"That's the one. Where is it?"

"Out back, but I need you to sign off on this. Gus can call you for a credit card." He shoved the repair order at her.

"You're sure it's okay with Gus that I take the car? Most places want payment first."

"Yeah, it's fine. Here," he said, handing her the keys. "Like I said, it's in the back."

She took them and stepped outside. "Now that was weird." She looked at Brooke and Amber. "No sense in you staying. I'll grab the car and be right behind you."

"No, I think we'd better go with you. Something doesn't seem right." Brooke glanced around, finding it odd that no other mechanics were in sight.

They walked to the back, not seeing the car, but spotting another building. The three made their way along the building, and turned at the end to see garage doors open on the back side.

"Is it just me, or is this pretty strange?" Dana asked as she looked into the opening to see her car inside. "There it is."

She walked toward it, her eyes adjusting to the lack of light with Brooke and Amber right behind her. They made it to the Jeep when they heard the sound of the door closing behind them.

"Well, guess we got a couple more than planned."

They turned to see a group of men, all in dark gear, standing near the door, blocking any exit. Dana couldn't think as her mind tried to process what was happening.

"Who are you and what do you want?" Dana asked, taking a few steps forward.

"We want Taylor's old lady, right there." Swinger pointed at Brooke, who gasped and took a step backward. "I guess we'll take all three of you." He nodded at the men around him. None were small, all were muscled, and not a one looked to have the least amount of compassion in their hard expressions.

"Now, here's how it's going to be. Two of the boys will drive your cars. You three will ride on the back with us."

"On your bikes?" Amber asked, feeling nauseous and wishing she'd listened to Eric.

"That's the idea. There'll be bikes all around us, so don't even think about jumping off or yelling for help. You do as I say and no one will get hurt."

"No." Brooke found her courage and stepped forward. "You're after my husband. Well, you won't get him through me." She crossed her arms and jutted her chin out.

Swinger moved to within inches of her, his menacing stare taking in her defiant stance. "It's good to have grit, but I guarantee you it won't save your old man." He grabbed her arm, pulling her toward him. "Kade sure knew how to attract the ladies. Maybe you and I can get together once he's out of the picture."

She tried to yank away, which caused him to grip her more tightly. "Never. Not ever, no matter what happens."

He laughed and shoved her toward the bikes lined against one wall before taking the car keys and tossing their purses inside the Jeep. "Mount up. Joker, you take the redhead, Tank, you get that one." Swinger pointed toward Amber. Their hands were tied in front of them before being lifted onto the bikes.

The bikers took off in the opposite direction from town, riding for a long time before turning onto a road almost hidden by overgrown trees and bushes. It seemed a miracle none of the three women fell off. They continued down the rutted road another ten minutes before pulling to a stop behind an old metal industrial building.

"Get off." Swinger jerked Brooke off the bike and pushed her forward toward a somewhat smaller building made of gray blocks. He shoved her through a metal door and held her upright as they stepped down a steep stairwell. Tank followed with Amber, and Joker with Dana. They walked down a narrow hallway before Swinger kicked open another metal door. The three were shoved inside before the door was slammed shut and locked, leaving them in darkness.

"Hey!" Dana yelled after them, anger and fear taking over as she looked around, trying to let her eyes adjust to the total darkness.

"Okay. Each of us move toward the door until we find each other." Amber's shaky, yet calm voice broke through the silence. "We can let our eyes adjust then decide if there's anything we can do."

"They took our phones...everything." Brooke wanted to scream, knowing it would do no good this far away from anyone.

Once they lowered themselves in front of the door, Amber worked at loosening the zip ties around her wrists without success.

"Eric and Kade will know something's wrong if we aren't back at the house by three," Amber said.

"It's after that now." Brooke also tried to loosen the ties before giving up.

"That means they're already in touch with Sheriff Andrews and Chief Towers. Plus J.D. and Clive. They'll find us." Amber's determination came from her complete faith in Eric's family— soon to be her family. They'd tear the town apart searching for them. "Kade just can't give himself over to them."

"They'll kill all of us whether he gives up or not. It's the way of it," Dana said, taking a deep breath. "One of the guys at work has a brother who's a one percent member. He has little to do with him, but he knows how they operate. None of it bodes well for us."

"You giving up?" Amber asked Dana.

"Hell no. I'll never give in to these bastards." Dana clenched her fists, trying to figure out what her father or brothers would do. Her father and mother retired from careers in the Army and her brothers were still in Special Forces. She'd inherited their toughness, their propensity to swear, as well as their never-give-up attitude.

"We need to find a way to get these ties off." Amber twisted her wrists, testing the strength once more.

"Can you reach in my back pocket?" Dana asked as she scooted with her back toward Amber.

"I think so." She reached a hand inside, feeling something hard touch her fingertips. "What is it?"

"A knife. I always carry a small pocket knife. Have since high school."

Amber pushed her hand further into the pocket, trying to get her fingers around it. She'd just gotten a grip with her thumb and forefinger when a lock clicked and the door began to push open, stopping when it hit their bodies.

"Get away from the door," Swinger growled.

They scooted away, moving toward one corner as the door opened and light illuminated the room from overhead. Swinger walked in, followed by Joker and Tank, who carried three bottles of water. He tossed them toward the women then stepped aside as Swinger lifted his phone and took several photos.

A moment later, a metal bed and mattress were brought in and shoved against a wall.

"Sit down. It won't be long before our boss is here to talk to you." Swinger started to turn.

"Robbie Morgan," Brooke said.

Swinger looked back at her. "Yes. And believe me, you will want to do everything he says." He shut the door, leaving the lone ceiling light on.

Chapter Twenty-Two

"I should've gone after them." Eric dragged his hands through his hair as Kade paced back and forth in the great room, listening to the conversations between the others. As soon as they had a location, he'd be on his bike and gone.

"Sheriff Andrews got a call from a business near the auto shop. He says three women walked into a back storage building then rode out with a group of bikers, followed by a yellow Jeep and red SUV." Clive knew there would be no holding Kade back once he learned where the women were being held—assuming they could figure it out. "Tip is there now, questioning someone who works at the auto shop, but he's too scared to talk. Sounds like the gang threatened him—"

"Or his family," Kade ground out. "Which way did they go?"

"Away from town. Tip has his deputies canvassing the area and Chief Towers added his officers to the hunt. J.D. and I are heading out that way now." Clive looked at Kade. "You aren't coming with us."

"The hell I'm not. They want me, and I won't sit around while they have our women. We'll figure it all out when we find them, but I'm not staying behind."

"I'm going." Eric grabbed his jacket.

"We're all going. Jace will ride with me." Heath pulled out his phone and sent a text before slipping it back in his pocket.

"I'm on my own." Kade walked outside without another word and climbed into his truck.

"No way he's out there alone," Mitch growled.

"Agreed," Eric answered as he and Mitch ran outside, hopping into Kade's truck, ignoring the anger on their brother's face.

"What the hell—"

"Deal with it, because we're not getting out." Eric buckled his seat belt and looked up to see J.D. and Clive pull out. "They're moving."

Kade let fly with a few choice oaths, then followed the agents off the ranch with Heath and Jace on their tail. The three vehicles parked next to a large van at the auto shop, which had been converted to a make-shift staging area. Tip Andrews and Buck Towers walked toward Clive and J.D., providing an update and glancing up when Heath, Jace, Eric, Kade, and Mitch joined them.

"This isn't a good place for you to be," Andrews said, knowing his plea would fall on deaf ears, yet hoping the men would go back home.

"We're here with three vehicles. What can we do?" Heath asked.

"Follow me." Andrews showed them a large map of the area, colorized with the names of those canvassing each section. "This is where we have the least coverage. There are hundreds of old roads, driveways, and abandoned buildings. It could take days or weeks to check all locations. My guess is they're hiding the women somewhere in here."

"We own land in this area." Jace pointed to a spot within the area the sheriff suggested they cover. He looked at Heath. "An old warehouse and block building our father built in the late 1950s." Jace glanced at Tip and Buck. "You know, when everyone was building fallout shelters. I haven't been by there for a couple of years."

"It would be just like Robbie to find property owned by the MacLarens and hide the hostages there. He'd find it ironic." Kade stared at the location. "It's as good a place as any to start."

******

Swinger opened the door and looked inside. The women sat together on the cot and fell silent as he stepped inside. He grabbed Brooke, hauling her in front of him.

"Do you have any idea what your old man had to do to earn the patches he wore?" He let out a cruel laugh. "I can see you don't. Well, let me tell you." He pulled her close and whispered in her ear, loud enough for Amber and Dana to hear. Brooke's eyes grew wide before tears began to form and she tried to jerk away. He shoved her back on the bed. "And you know what else, the brothers watched." He walked to the door. "Now you three behave. There's someone coming to talk with you and I don't want you giving him any of your lip." He slammed the door behind him, the sound of the lock sliding into place ringing in their ears.

Amber scooted over next to her, pain flowing through her at what Swinger had told Brooke. "It's going to be all right. We'll figure a way out of this, and when we do, we'll put it all behind us. What we learned here will stay in

287

these walls—forever." She looked at Dana who nodded.

"After I kill as many of them as I can." Brooke's words were barely discernable, but Amber had no doubt if Brooke had a weapon, she'd do all she could to make good on her vow.

Swinger ascended the stairs just as Robbie and three others stopped their bikes and got off.

"They downstairs?"

"Right where you want them, Robbie. Downstairs at the far back corner." Swinger answered as they walked toward the cement block building. "Taylor's old lady and two others. All three live on the ranch, so the other two must be connected to the MacLarens."

Robbie looked around at the hidden location, wondering how long it would take Taylor to figure out they were hiding right in the middle of MacLaren property. They'd always told each other the best hiding places were those no one would figure to look because they were just too obvious. Robbie had no doubt Taylor would figure it out, even if no one else did—and he'd come for his old lady.

"All right. Let's go." Robbie descended the stairs, trudged down the hallway to the last door, and stopped.

Most of the brothers had no problem using women as hostages. He did. It became a last resort for him, except in this case, he looked forward to the look on Kade's face when he got a glimpse of his old lady in captivity. It wouldn't be pretty. Robbie knew his ex-brother would make the exchange right there. They'd already planned to leave the three women, taking just the man they came for, who would disappear on their way north.

Robbie turned the knob and pushed the door open, stepping into a room that smelled stale from the musty, damp air. Three women huddled together on a small bed.

"Which one?"

Swinger pointed to Brooke. "The blonde."

Robbie stopped in front of her to look into hostile eyes full of intelligence—and fear.

"Boys tell me your name is Brooke. Looks like you're the key to getting Taylor to come to us." He reached out, grasping strands of her hair, and letting them slide through his fingers. "I never knew him to be attracted to regular citizens. His tastes ran tough and hard, toward women who could deal with his demands. That you, sugar? A woman who can deal with a man like him?"

Brooke tried to turn away, but his grip tightened enough to cause her to wince in pain.

"Back off. What do you expect her to say with you looming over her?" Dana glared at Robbie, defiance flashing in her eyes.

He looked over at her, a grim smile on his face. "What's your name, sugar?"

Amber's eyes widened at the endearment he'd used twice, and looked at Dana. "You don't need to tell him. Let him figure it out."

Robbie let go of Brooke to grab Amber's chin, tilting her face toward him. She refused to meet his gaze, shaking her head violently. His grip tightened, forcing her to look up at him.

"I don't know who you two are and I don't fuckin' care. You can stay in this room and rot, 'cause no one's likely to ever find you once we leave. You play nice and we just might let someone know about you. You get me?"

Amber nodded, then glanced at the floor when he let go of her chin.

"Here's how it will be. There's no doubt in my mind Taylor will show up. We'll trade his old lady for him and leave you two here as security until we get away. In the meantime, nothing will happen to you—if you behave."

Amber stared at him, the cadence of his voice washing over her.

"What the hell do you expect us to do? Run?" Dana tried to stand, but Robbie pushed her back on the bed.

Robbie looked over his shoulder at Swinger, a feral gleam in his eyes. "Maybe I'll change my mind and we'll take this one with us. What do you think?"

Swinger leaned against the wall, cracking his knuckles, looking bored. "She's a fireball, that's for sure. She might make a good club whore." His chuckle caused the hairs on Dana's neck to bristle. She'd heard the term—a woman made available to all club members—and knew she'd rather be dead than forced to live like that.

"Never," she ground out, eyes flashing.

Amber continued to stare at him, fear and confusion mixing in her mind.

Robbie let his eyes wander over each of the women once more, then settled his gaze on Dana. "You know what, sugar? You just might like it." He turned toward the door and took a couple of steps.

"Daddy..." a voice behind him breathed out, so low he almost missed it. He stopped, going completely still at the sound and pitch of the strained voice. He turned around to look at the three.

"Who said that?" He moved closer, taking another hard look at each.

"I...did."

His gaze shot to the one in the middle with mahogany colored hair and jade green eyes with gold flecks. His breath hitched as he stared into those eyes.

"What's your name, sugar?" His voice sounded odd and shaky.

"Amber."

His features froze as his heartbeat seemed to stop. He dropped to one knee, cupping her face in his hands, noting every feature, wanting to make certain. He grabbed the hem of her blouse and yanked it up, ignoring the shouts of the other two women, and searched for something. His eyes landed on a small birthmark, a star, just to the right of her belly button. He dropped her blouse and grabbed her by her bound wrists, pulling her up, leading her from the room.

"What the hell, Robbie?" Swinger asked, afraid he already knew the answer.

Robbie looked over his shoulder. "You and Joker watch those two. No one else comes down here except us three. You got me?"

"Yeah, I got you." Swinger didn't like it one bit, but he'd do anything for Robbie, even give his life for the man. Which he might have to do before this was done.

Robbie opened the door to a room at the base of the stairs and pulled Amber inside. He turned her toward him, pulled out a knife, and cut the zip tie. She rubbed her wrists, not taking her eyes from the man she knew to be her birth father. The man who'd walked away from her when she was seven and never returned.

He paced a few feet away, dragging a hand through his hair, then placing fisted hands on his hips. He spun toward her.

"What the hell am I going to do with you?"

"Is that all you have to say to me after all these years?"

The sadness in her voice almost brought him to his knees. She wanted answers. He had none, at least nothing he could use to justify his actions years before. He'd been vulnerable when his father, Sonny, forced him to give up the only person in his life who'd ever mattered—Amber.

"I saw you playing softball at school once. You were about thirteen. I knew you'd turn into a beauty, and you have."

"You saw me? Why didn't you say anything?" She took a step toward him then stopped, clasping her hands in front of her.

"I wasn't supposed to know where you were living or who adopted you. My friend in social services in Wyoming told me, but made me promise I'd never approach you without going through her. She died the next year." His voice held the sadness of a man who'd bottled up the loss of his daughter for over twenty years, telling himself he'd had no other choice. "Your adopted family moved shortly afterwards. I was never able to find you again and decided it was for the best. You were happy, with a good family, you didn't need someone like me messing in your life." He leaned his back against a wall and slid to the floor, resting his elbows on his knees.

She sat down next to him and took his hand in hers. "You were a good father. I missed you." Her voice broke as she remembered the man who played dress up with her, took her for ice cream, and let her watch scary movies. She leaned toward him, resting her head on his shoulder.

Robbie wrapped an arm around her, pulling her close, and placed a kiss on the top of her head. Amber being here changed everything.

"What do the other two women mean to you?"

"I've known Kade's wife, Brooke, since high school. I dated her younger brother, Eric

Sinclair. He's my fiancé." She held up her left hand so Robbie could see the ring. "Dana is my closest friend. She's like a sister to me. They're all like family to me." She took a shaky breath as she drew away from him. "What are you going to do?"

Robbie knew his life would be worthless if he didn't eliminate Kade. His father would order him hunted down and killed, maybe by those closest to him—Swinger and Joker. The appearance of his daughter after all this time messed with what had been an easy plan. He'd been a club member his entire adult life, knew the consequences of betraying his brothers, and had sacrificed much to attain the presidency. Now, none of it seemed important. Amber, sitting alongside him, finally back in his life, meant more to him than any vendetta or order from a man sitting in a prison cell. He squeezed her one more time and placed a kiss on her forehead, then stood, reaching out a hand to help her up.

"I don't know." He looked at her again, his heart breaking at what a beautiful woman she'd become. "You won't like it, but you need to stay in here until I've sorted it all out." Robbie opened the door and walked out.

"Wait—" Amber called as the door closed, the lock clicking in place. She shut her eyes tight, praying he'd give up his revenge and send them home. She slid back down to the floor, leaned against the wall, and rested her head back, hoping she'd know something soon.

Chapter Twenty-Three

"Pack up. We're getting out of here before Taylor and the others show up."

Robbie stood next to his brothers as the sun began to set over the nearby mountains. The temperature would drop rapidly once the sun disappeared.

"What the hell? We can't ignore a direct order from Sonny, or let a brother live who's betrayed the club. You know the rules and the consequences better than any of us." Swinger stood a foot from Robbie, as close as he dared get without setting off a direct confrontation with his president.

"Things have changed." Robbie moved toward his bike, slipping a heavy jacket over his cut.

"Bullshit. We're committed to this." Swinger stood behind him, angry and confused.

Robbie turned to see a .38 pointed at him. "You want to shoot me, Swinger? Then do it. My order as the national president is to get our asses out of here. Leave them for the law to find." He took a step forward, crowding Swinger. "That's my daughter in there, the MacLarens and Sinclairs are her family. You'll have to kill me if you intend to go after any of them."

"And Sonny?"

"He's in jail. We're clean. We can ride out, continue our businesses, and forget the past. The way Joker's got the numbers figured, we'll all be multi-millionaires within the year. If we kill Kade, we'll be nothing but fugitives, always trying to stay ahead of those who'll hunt us." He looked around at the other brothers then glared at the man in front of him. "I'm going to say goodbye to my daughter, then I'm gone." He shoved past Swinger and dashed down the stairs.

Amber looked up as the door opened and Robbie walked in. She pushed up from the floor and waited, swallowing the lump in her throat.

"We're leaving. The cars are outside with your purses and phones." He pursed his lips and started to leave.

"Daddy...wait." She dashed up to him, threw her arms around his neck, and held on. "Don't leave me. Not again."

Robbie could hear the desperation in her voice, her heart breaking the same as his. He wrapped his arms around her, wishing his decision to leave could be different.

"I have to go, sugar. You and I both know that." He kissed her on the forehead and dropped his arms. "Tell Kade it's over."

"When will I see you again?" She swiped at tears, still not believing he'd walk away from her again.

"Oh, I'll be around, sugar. I'll always be close by if you need me." He offered her a hesitant smile then took off up the stairs, swung onto his bike, noting the others were already mounted and ready to leave. "Let's go." He pulled out, not looking back, knowing she stood outside watching him go.

"No..." she whispered, knowing he wouldn't stop. Amber watched as they took a different road out, heading north, away from Fire Mountain. She wrapped her arms around her waist, taking a few hesitant steps, then stopped, realizing any effort to stop him would be futile.

Amber stood until the rumbling sounds of the bikes disappeared. To her left she saw clouds of dust coming up the same road where they rode in hours before.

"There, up ahead. It looks like Amber." Eric jumped from the truck before Kade could stop, ran to her and wrapped her in his arms.

Kade and Mitch hurried up to them "Where's Brooke and Dana?" Kade demanded.

She pointed toward the open door. "Down the stairs. They're in a room at the end of the hall." She glanced up at Eric, tightening her arms around him, and began to cry. Gulping sobs that wracked her body.

"It's all right, baby. They're gone." Eric tried to soothe her, believing it was relief causing the strong reaction.

"He's gone," she sobbed into his chest.

"I know, baby."

She shook her head. "My father's gone, Eric. He did it for me."

Eric began to speak when Kade walked outside with Brooke, followed by Dana and Mitch. Amber broke away and ran toward them.

"My God. He's your father?" Dana asked, wrapping her arms around Amber.

The men shot startled looks at each other as the sheriff and police chief pulled up.

"Yes. My biological father." She swiped at more tears, wiping the moisture on her jeans. "I haven't seen him since he gave me up when I was seven."

Eric clasped her shoulder, turning Amber toward him. "Robbie Morgan is your father?"

She nodded. "And now he's gone. Again."

"I'll be damned," Kade mumbled, pulling Brooke close to his side.

Mitch watched Dana shiver, her lips turning blue. He slipped off his jacket and held it out to her. "Here, put this on. You're turning to ice."

"Let's get out of here," Eric suggested. "You can explain what happened to everyone at one time."

******

"That's the final decision, Kade?" Clive asked.

Kade nodded, looking around at the members of his family for confirmation.

"And you're okay with it?" J.D. asked him, uneasy that no one would step forward and press charges.

"Yes. The way I understand it, Robbie came to town to visit his daughter, Amber, then took off before the weather turned. Done deal." He crossed his arms over his chest and grinned at his ex-colleagues.

"And you don't know how to reach him, is that correct, Amber?" Sheriff Andrews asked.

"He didn't give me an address or phone number, if that's what you're asking." She stood in front of Eric, his arms wrapped around her waist. "However, I'm certain Agents Montalban and Nelson can find some way to contact him, if needed."

Andrews shook his head and chuckled. "Yes, I'm sure they can find a way. Guess there's not much more we can do. According to the women, no crime seems to have occurred. Now, about the costs?" Tip set down his pen and looked at Heath.

"I'm certain we can work something out, Sheriff." Heath shook his hand, then Chief Tower's before turning toward his family. "I think it's time we all headed home."

Epilogue

Three months later...

"Here's to your one month anniversary. Hope you have many, many more." Kade raised his glass to Eric and Amber, hearing the cheers of those standing around the reception tent outside the ranch house.

Eric pulled his wife into a hug then lowered his mouth to hers in a searing kiss, which prompted more cheers and applause. They'd had a quiet ceremony a month after Robbie rode out of town. Amber's parents arrived from their home in Florida to attend the nuptials, her father pushing her mother in her wheelchair—at least they'd made it. They'd flown back for the reception, this time with her brothers, Ryan and Jake.

"Do you think you'll ever hear from him again?" Dana handed Amber a glass of wine, taking a sip from her own glass as she listened to the band play a popular country song.

"I don't know. I hope so." She let out a deep sigh as the image of Robbie riding away floated across her memory. Over the weeks she'd come to think of him more as Robbie Morgan than as her birth father—the man who'd help conceive her. "It's a strange miracle we met up at all."

"You're lucky. You have a family who loves you." Dana nodded toward Amber's parents, the ones who raised her.

Amber's mouth curved into a smile. "You're right. I'm truly fortunate. Tell me how you like your newest job."

"It's good and the owners are wonderful. They keep me busy with new projects and it helps pay the bills." She'd gotten the job at the advertising agency. That, plus continuing projects through Amber and her two classes at the college kept her busy. "What's the deal on your honeymoon?"

"We leave in three days, and I can't wait." Amber waved to her brother, Jake, who stood next to Kade, no doubt talking Army speak. Jake graduated from West Point and Kade left Special Ops to join the DEA. She knew they'd bond.

"Where to?" Dana watched Mitch pick up another beer while talking to a tall, dark-haired woman she'd never seen. She winced as he threw his head back and laughed at something the woman said. For the first time she realized she'd never heard the man laugh—not once in all these months. They'd been around each other often since Robbie left town, each time tense and difficult. Dana would be glad when he left for Montana.

"I don't know. Eric is surprising me." Amber's gaze settled on her husband, her heart skipping a beat as it always did when he was around. She watched as he set down his glass and walked over to her, taking her hand in his.

"May I have this dance?"

"Anytime," she laughed.

Dana watched from the sidelines. So many lives had changed over the last few months, hers included. She loved Fire Mountain and looked forward to riding the new Harley she'd purchased a week ago over all the winding roads. Her eyes scanned the crowd, not seeing Mitch this time, then shifting her gaze as he came into sight on the dance floor, holding the dark-haired woman in a tight embrace, swaying to the music. She caught his eye, raised her glass in salute, then turned to leave.

Mitch held his partner, half listening to what she said as his gaze wandered to Dana. She stood next to Amber, leaned up and gave her a kiss on the cheek, then set her drink down and walked away. A moment later he spotted her heading toward the parking area. He didn't know why, but he wished she was the one on the dance floor with him instead of the woman in his arms.

He shook his head at the foolish thought. They were oil and water. Nothing about her appealed to him from her red hair and freckles to her pushy personality. Besides, he'd be leaving for Montana in a few weeks after completing his training at company headquarters. They'd see each other rarely, which was fine with him.

The dance ended and he turned his attention toward the sound of a motorcycle starting up. He spotted the big, copper and black Harley right off, admiring its lines. Then his eyes moved up to the rider and the can of beer he'd picked up slipped from his grip. Skirt pulled up to her thighs, bright copper and black helmet on her head, and red strands of hair peeking out from underneath. His breath caught and his mouth went dry at the sight.

As the dust from her cycle settled and she disappeared down the drive, Mitch knew the time had come to leave Fire Mountain and a certain redhead far behind.

Join me in the continuation of the MacLarens of Fire Mountain Contemporary series with the story of Mitch and Dana in book six, Hearts Don't Lie, due to release in 2015.

Thank you for taking the time to read Always Love You. If you enjoyed it, please consider telling your friends or posting a short review. Word of mouth is an author's best friend and much appreciated.

Please join my reader's group to be notified of my New Releases at:
http://www.shirleendavies.com/contact-me.html

I care about quality, so if you find something in error, please contact me via email at
shirleen@shirleendavies.com

About the Author

Shirleen Davies writes romance—historical, contemporary, and romantic suspense. She grew up in Southern California, attended Oregon State University, and has degrees from San Diego State University and the University of Maryland. During the day she provides consulting services to small and mid-sized businesses. But her real passion is writing emotionally charged stories of flawed people who find redemption through love and acceptance. She now lives with her husband in a beautiful town in northern Arizona.

Shirleen loves to hear from her readers.

Write to her at: shirleen@shirleendavies.com
Visit her website:
http://www.shirleendavies.com
Sign up to be notified of New Releases:
http://www.shirleendavies.com/contact-me.html

Comment on her blog:
http://www.shirleendavies.com/blog.html
Facebook Fan Page:
https://www.facebook.com/ShirleenDaviesAuthor
Twitter: http://twitter.com/shirleendavies
Google+:
   http://www.gplusid.com/shirleendavies
LinkedIn:
   http://www.linkedin.com/in/shirleendaviesauthor
Pinterest:
   http://www.pinterest.com/shirleendavies
Tsu: http://www.tsu.co/shirleendavies

Other Books by Shirleen Davies

http://www.shirleendavies.com/books.html

Tougher than the Rest – Book One
MacLarens of Fire Mountain Historical Western Romance Series
"A passionate, fast-paced story set in the untamed western frontier by an exciting new voice in historical romance."
Niall MacLaren is the oldest of four brothers, and the undisputed leader of the family. A widower, and single father, his focus is on building the MacLaren ranch into the largest and most successful in northern Arizona. He is serious about two things—his responsibility to the family and his future marriage to the wealthy, well-connected widow who will secure his place in the territory's destiny.

Katherine is determined to live the life she's dreamed about. With a job waiting for her in the growing town of Los Angeles, California, the young teacher from Philadelphia begins a journey across the United States with only a couple of trunks and her spinster companion. Life is perfect for this adventurous, beautiful young woman, until an accident throws her into the arms of the one man who can destroy it all.

Fighting his growing attraction and strong desire for the beautiful stranger, Niall is more determined than ever to push emotions aside to focus on his goals of wealth and political gain. But looking into the clear, blue eyes of the woman who could ruin everything, Niall discovers he will have to harden his heart and be tougher than he's ever been in his life...Tougher than the Rest.

Faster than the Rest – Book Two
MacLarens of Fire Mountain Historical Western Romance Series
"Headstrong, brash, confident, and complex, the MacLarens of Fire Mountain will captivate you with strong characters set in the wild and rugged western frontier."
Handsome, ruthless, young U.S. Marshal Jamie MacLaren had lost everything—his parents, his family connections, and his childhood sweetheart—but now he's back in Fire Mountain and ready for another chance. Just as he successfully reconnects with his family and starts to rebuild his life, he gets the unexpected and unwanted assignment of rescuing the woman who broke his heart.

Beautiful, wealthy Victoria Wicklin chose money and power over love, but is now fighting for her life—or is she? Who has she become in the seven years since she left Fire Mountain to take up her life in San Francisco? Is she really as innocent as she says?

Marshal MacLaren struggles to learn the truth and do his job, but the past and present lead him in different directions as his heart and brain wage battle. Is Victoria a victim or a villain? Is life offering him another chance, or just another heartbreak?

As Jamie and Victoria struggle to uncover past secrets and come to grips with their shared passion, another danger arises. A life-altering danger that is out of their control and threatens to destroy any chance for a shared future.

Harder than the Rest – Book Three
MacLarens of Fire Mountain Historical Western Romance Series
"They are men you want on your side. Hard, confident, and loyal, the MacLarens of Fire Mountain will seize your attention from the first page."
Will MacLaren is a hardened, plain-speaking bounty hunter. His life centers on finding men guilty of horrendous crimes and making sure justice is done. There is no place in his world for

the carefree attitude he carried years before when a tragic event destroyed his dreams.

Amanda is the daughter of a successful Colorado rancher. Determined and proud, she works hard to prove she is as capable as any man and worthy to be her father's heir. When a stranger arrives, her independent nature collides with the strong pull toward the handsome ranch hand. But is he what he seems and could his secrets endanger her as well as her family?

The last thing Will needs is to feel passion for another woman. But Amanda elicits feelings he thought were long buried. Can Will's desire for her change him? Or will the vengeance he seeks against the one man he wants to destroy—a dangerous opponent without a conscious—continue to control his life?

Stronger than the Rest – Book Four
MacLarens of Fire Mountain Historical Western Romance Series
"Smart, tough, and capable, the MacLarens protect their own no matter the odds. Set against America's rugged frontier, the stories of the men from Fire Mountain are complex, fast-paced, and a must read for anyone who enjoys non-stop action and romance."
Drew MacLaren is focused and strong. He has achieved all of his goals except one—to return to

the MacLaren ranch and build the best horse breeding program in the west. His successful career as an attorney is about to give way to his ranching roots when a bullet changes everything.

Tess Taylor is the quiet, serious daughter of a Colorado ranch family with dreams of her own. Her shy nature keeps her from developing friendships outside of her close-knit family until Drew enters her life. Their relationship grows. Then a bullet, meant for another, leaves him paralyzed and determined to distance himself from the one woman he's come to love.

Convinced he is no longer the man Tess needs, Drew focuses on regaining the use of his legs and recapturing a life he thought lost. But danger of another kind threatens those he cares about—including Tess—forcing him to rethink his future.

Can Drew overcome the barriers that stand between him, the safety of his friends and family, and a life with the woman he loves? To do it all, he has to be strong. Stronger than the Rest.

Deadlier than the Rest – Book Five
MacLarens of Fire Mountain Historical Western Romance Series
"A passionate, heartwarming story of the iconic MacLarens of Fire Mountain.

Connor MacLaren's search has already stolen eight years of his life. Now he is close to finding what he seeks—Meggie, his missing sister. His quest leads him to the growing city of Salt Lake and an encounter with the most captivating woman he has ever met.

Grace is the third wife of a Mormon farmer, forced into a life far different from what she'd have chosen. Her independent spirit longs for choices governed only by her own heart and mind. To achieve her dreams, she must hide behind secrets and half-truths, even as her heart pulls her towards the ruggedly handsome Connor.

Known as cool and uncompromising, Connor MacLaren lives by a few, firm rules that have served him well and kept him alive. However, danger stalks Connor, even to the front range of the beautiful Wasatch Mountains, threatening those he cares about and impacting his ability to find his sister.

Can Connor protect himself from those who seek his death? Will his eight-year search lead him to his sister while unlocking the secrets he knows are held tight within Grace, the woman who has captured his heart?

Read this heartening story of duty, honor, passion, and love in book five of the MacLarens of Fire Mountain series.

Wilder than the Rest – Book Six
MacLarens of Fire Mountain Historical Western Romance Series

"A captivating historical western romance set in the burgeoning and treacherous city of San Francisco. Go along for the ride in this gripping story that seizes your attention from the very first page."

"If you're a reader who wants to discover an entire family of characters you can fall in love with, this is the series for you." – Authors to Watch

Pierce is a rough man, but happy in his new life as a Special Agent. Tasked with defending the rights of the federal government, Pierce is a cunning gunslinger always ready to tackle the next job. That is, until he finds out that his new job involves Mollie Jamison.

Mollie can be a lot to handle. Headstrong and independent, Mollie has chosen a life of danger and intrigue guaranteed to prove her liquor-loving father wrong. She will make something of herself, and no one, not even arrogant Pierce MacLaren, will stand in her way.

A secret mission brings them together, but will their attraction to each other prove deadly in their hunt for justice? The payoff for success is high, much higher than any assignment either has taken before. But will the damage to their hearts and souls be too much to bear? Can Pierce and Mollie find a way to overcome their misgivings and work together as one?

Second Summer – Book One
**MacLarens of Fire Mountain
Contemporary Romance Series**
"In this passionate Contemporary Romance, author Shirleen Davies introduces her readers to the modern day MacLarens starting with Heath MacLaren, the head of the family."
The Chairman of both the MacLaren Cattle Co. and MacLaren Land Development, Heath MacLaren is a success professionally—his personal life is another matter.
Following a divorce after a long, loveless marriage, Heath spends his time with women who are beautiful and passionate, yet unable to provide what he longs for . . .

Heath has never experienced love even though he witnesses it every day between his younger brother, Jace, and wife, Caroline. He wants what they have, yet spends his time with women too young to understand what drives him and too focused on themselves to be true companions.

It's been two years since Annie's husband died, leaving her to build a new life. He was her soul mate and confidante. She has no desire to find a replacement, yet longs for male friendship.

Annie's closest friend in Fire Mountain, Caroline MacLaren, is determined to see Annie come out of her shell after almost two years of mourning. A chance meeting with Heath turns into an offer to be a part of the MacLaren Foundation Board and an opportunity for a life outside her home sanctuary which has also become her prison. The platonic friendship that builds between Annie and Heath points to a future where each may rely on the other without the bonds a romance would entail.

However, without consciously seeking it, each yearns for more . . .

The MacLaren Development Company is booming with Heath at the helm. His meetings at a partner company with the young, beautiful marketing director, who makes no secret of her desire for him, are a temptation. But is she the type of woman he truly wants?

Annie's acceptance of the deep, yet passionless, friendship with Heath sustains her, lulling her to believe it is all she needs. At least until Heath drops a bombshell, forcing Annie to realize that what she took for friendship is actually a deep, lasting love. One she doesn't want to lose.

Each must decide to settle—or fight for it all.

Hard Landing – Book Two
MacLarens of Fire Mountain
Contemporary Romance Series

Trey MacLaren is a confident, poised Navy pilot. He's focused, loyal, ethical, and a natural leader. He is also on his way to what he hopes will be a lasting relationship and marriage with fellow pilot, Jesse Evans.

Jesse has always been driven. Her graduation from the Naval Academy and acceptance into the pilot training program are all she thought she wanted—until she discovered love with Trey MacLaren

Trey and Jesse's lives are filled with fast flying, friends, and the demands of their military careers. Lives each has settled into with a passion. At least until the day Trey receives a letter that could change his and Jesse's lives forever.

It's been over two years since Trey has seen the woman in Pensacola. Her unexpected letter stuns him and pushes Jesse into a tailspin from which she might not pull back.

Each must make a choice. Will the choice Trey makes cause him to lose Jesse forever? Will she follow her heart or her head as she fights for a chance to save the love she's found? Will their independent decisions collide, forcing them to give up on a life together?

One More Day – Book Three
MacLarens of Fire Mountain Contemporary Romance Series

Cameron "Cam" Sinclair is smart, driven, and dedicated, with an easygoing temperament that belies his strong will and the personal ambitions he holds close. Besides his family, his job as head of IT at the MacLaren Cattle Company and his position as a Search and Rescue volunteer are all he needs to make him happy. At least that's what he thinks until he meets, and is instantly drawn to, fellow SAR volunteer, Lainey Devlin.

Lainey is compassionate, independent, and ready to break away from her manipulative and controlling fiancé. Just as her decision is made, she's called into a major search and rescue effort, where once again, her path crosses with the intriguing, and much too handsome, Cam Sinclair. But Lainey's plans are set. An opportunity to buy a flourishing preschool in northern Arizona is her chance to make a fresh start, and nothing, not even her fierce attraction to Cam Sinclair, will impede her plans.

As Lainey begins to settle into her new life, an unexpected danger arises —threats from an unknown assailant—someone who doesn't believe she belongs in Fire Mountain. The more Lainey begins to love her new home, the greater the danger becomes. Can she accept the help and protection Cam offers while ignoring her consuming desire for him?

Even if Lainey accepts her attraction to Cam, will he ever be able to come to terms with his own driving ambition and allow himself to consider a different life than the one he's always pictured? A life with the one woman who offers more than he'd ever hoped to find?

All Your Nights – Book Four
MacLarens of Fire Mountain Contemporary Romance Series
"Romance, adventure, cowboys, suspense—everything you want in a contemporary western romance novel."
Kade Taylor likes living on the edge. As an undercover agent for the DEA and a former Special Ops team member, his current assignment seems tame—keep tabs on a bookish Ph.D. candidate the agency believes is connected to a ruthless drug cartel.

Brooke Sinclair is weeks away from obtaining her goal of a doctoral degree. She spends time finalizing her presentation and relaxing with another student who seems to want nothing more than her friendship. That's fine with

Brooke. Her last serious relationship ended in a broken engagement.

Her future is set, safe and peaceful, just as she's always planned—until Agent Taylor informs her she's under suspicion for illegal drug activities.

Kade and his DEA team obtain evidence which exonerates Brooke while placing her in danger from those who sought to use her. As Kade races to take down the drug cartel while protecting Brooke, he must also find common ground with the former suspect—a woman he desires with increasing intensity.

At odds with her better judgment, Brooke finds the more time she spends with Kade, the more she's attracted to the complex, multi-faceted agent. But Kade holds secrets he knows Brooke will never understand or accept.

Can Kade keep Brooke safe while coming to terms with his past, or will he stay silent, ruining any future with the woman his heart can't let go?

Always Love You– Book Five
MacLarens of Fire Mountain
Contemporary Romance Series
"Romance, adventure, motorcycles, cowboys, suspense—everything you

want in a contemporary western romance novel."

Eric Sinclair loves his bachelor status. His work at MacLaren Enterprises leaves him with plenty of time to ride his horse as well as his Harley...and date beautiful women without a thought to commitment.

Amber Anderson is the new person at MacLaren Enterprises. Her passion for marketing landed her what she believes to be the perfect job—until she steps into her first meeting to find the man she left, but still loves, sitting at the management table—his disdain for her clear.

Eric won't allow the past to taint his professional behavior, nor will he repeat his mistakes with Amber, even though love for her pulses through him as strong as ever.

As they strive to mold a working relationship, unexpected danger confronts those close to them, pitting the MacLarens and Sinclairs against an evil who stalks one member but threatens them all.

Eric can't get the memories of their passionate past out of his mind, while Amber wrestles with feelings she thought long buried. Will they be able to put the past behind them to reclaim the love lost years before?

Hearts Don't Lie– Book Six
MacLarens of Fire Mountain
Contemporary Romance Series

Mitch MacLaren has reasons for avoiding relationships, and in his opinion, they're pretty darn good. As the new president of RTC Bucking Bulls, difficult challenges occur daily. He certainly doesn't need another one in the form of a fiery, blue-eyed, redhead.

Dana Ballard's new job forces her to work with the one MacLaren who can't seem to get over himself and lighten up. Their verbal sparring is second nature and entertaining until the night of Mitch's departure when he surprises her with a dare she doesn't refuse.

With his assignment in Fire Mountain over, Mitch is free to return to Montana and run the business his father helped start. The glitch in his enthusiasm has to do with one irreversible mistake—the dare Dana didn't ignore. Now, for reasons that confound him, he just can't let it go.

Working together is a circumstance neither wants, but both must accept. As their attraction grows, so do the accidents and strange illnesses of the animals RTC depends on to stay in business. Mitch's total focus should be on finding the reasons and people behind the incidents. Instead, he finds himself torn between his unwanted desire for Dana and the business which is his life.

In his mind, a simple proposition can solve one problem. Will Dana make the smart move and walk away? Or take the gamble and expose her heart?

No Getting Over You– Book Seven
MacLarens of Fire Mountain Contemporary Romance Series
Cassie MacLaren has come a long way since being dumped by her long-time boyfriend, a man she believed to be her future. Successful in her job at MacLaren Enterprises, dreaming of one day leading one of the divisions, she's moved on to start a new relationship, having little time to dwell on past mistakes.

Matt Garner loves his job as rodeo representative for Double Ace Bucking Stock. Busy days and constant travel leave no time for anything more than the occasional short-term relationship—which is just the way he likes it. He's come to accept the regret of leaving the woman he loved for the pro rodeo circuit.
The future is set for both, until a chance meeting ignites long buried emotions neither is willing to face.

Forced to work together, their attraction grows, even as multiple arson fires threaten Cassie's new home of Cold Creek, Colorado. Although Cassie believes the danger from the fires is remote, she knows the danger Matt poses to her heart is real.

While fighting his renewed feelings for Cassie, Matt focuses on a new and unexpected opportunity offered by MacLaren Enterprises— an opportunity that will put him on a direct collision course with Cassie.

Will pride and self-preservation control their future? Or will one be strong enough to make the first move, risking everything, including their heart?

Redemption's Edge – Book One
Redemption Mountain – Historical Western Romance Series
"A heartwarming, passionate story of loss, forgiveness, and redemption set in the untamed frontier during the tumultuous years following the Civil War. Ms. Davies' engaging and complex characters draw you in from the start, creating an exciting introduction to this new historical western romance series."

Dax Pelletier is ready for a new life, far away from the one he left behind in Savannah following the South's devastating defeat in the Civil War. The ex-Confederate general wants nothing more to do with commanding men and confronting the tough truths of leadership.

Rachel Davenport possesses skills unlike those of her Boston socialite peers—skills honed as a nurse in field hospitals during the Civil War. Eschewing her northeastern suitors and changed by the carnage she's seen, Rachel decides to accept her uncle's invitation to assist him at his clinic in the dangerous and wild frontier of Montana.

Now a Texas Ranger, a promise to a friend takes Dax and his brother, Luke, to the untamed territory of Montana. He'll fulfill his oath and return to Austin, at least that's what he believes.

The small town of Splendor is what Rachel needs after life in a large city. In a few short months, she's grown to love the people as well as the majestic beauty of the untamed frontier. She's settled into a life unlike any she has ever thought possible.

Thinking his battle days are over, he now faces dangers of a different kind—one by those from his past who seek vengeance, and another from Rachel, the woman who's captured his heart.

Wildfire Creek – Book Two
Redemption Mountain – Historical Western Romance Series
"A passionate story of rebuilding lives, working to find a place in the wild frontier, and building new lives in the years following the American Civil War. A rugged, heartwarming story of choices and love in the continuing saga of Redemption Mountain."

Luke Pelletier is settling into his new life as a rancher and occasional Pinkerton Agent, leaving his past as an ex-Confederate major and Texas Ranger far behind. He wants nothing more than to work the ranch, charm the ladies, and live a life of carefree bachelorhood.

Ginny Sorensen has accepted her responsibility as the sole provider for herself and her younger sister. The desire to continue their journey to Oregon is crushed when the need for food and shelter keeps them in the growing frontier town of Splendor, Montana, forcing Ginny to accept work as a server in the local saloon.

Luke has never met a woman as lovely and unspoiled as Ginny. He longs to know her, yet fears his wild ways and unsettled nature aren't what she deserves. She's a girl you marry, but that is nowhere in Luke's plans.

Complicating their tenuous friendship, a twist in circumstances forces Ginny closer to the man she most wants to avoid—the man who can destroy her dreams, and who's captured her heart.

Believing his bachelor status firm, Luke moves from danger to adventure, never dreaming each step he takes brings him closer to his true destiny and a life much different from what he imagines.

Sunrise Ridge – Book Three
Redemption Mountain – Historical Western Romance Series

"The author has a talent for bringing the historical west to life, realistically and vividly, and doesn't shy away from some of the harder aspects of frontier life, even though it's fiction. Recommended to readers who like sweeping western historical romances that are grounded with memorable, likeable characters and a strong sense of place."

Noah Brandt is a successful blacksmith and businessman in Splendor, Montana, with few ties to his past as an ex-Union Army major and sharpshooter. Quiet and hardworking, his

biggest challenge is controlling his strong desire
for a woman he believes is beyond his reach.
Abigail Tolbert is tired of being under her
father's thumb while at the same time, being
pushed away by the one man she desires.
Determined to build a new life outside the
control of her wealthy father, she finds work and
sets out to shape a life on her own terms.

Noah has made too many mistakes with Abby
to have any hope of getting her back. Even with
the changes in her life, including the distance
she's built with her father, he can't keep himself
from believing he'll never be good enough to
claim her.

Unexpected dangers, including a twist of fate
for Abby, change both their lives, making the
tentative steps they've taken to build a
relationship a distant hope. As Noah battles his
past as well as the threats to Abby, she fights for
a future with the only man she will ever love.

Dixie Moon – Book Four
Redemption Mountain – Historical Western Romance Series

Gabe Evans is a man of his word with strong
convictions and steadfast loyalty. As the sheriff
of Splendor, Montana, the ex-Union Colonel and
oldest of four boys from an affluent family, Gabe
understands the meaning of responsibility. The

last thing he wants is another commitment—especially of the female variety.

Until he meets Lena Campanel...

Lena's past is one she intends to keep buried. Overcoming a childhood of setbacks and obstacles, she and her friend, Nick, have succeeded in creating a life of financial success and devout loyalty to one another.

When an unexpected death leaves Gabe the sole heir of a considerable estate, partnering with Nick and Lena is a lucrative decision...forcing Gabe and Lena to work together. As their desire grows, Lena refuses to let down her guard, vowing to keep her past hidden—even from a perfect man like Gabe.

But secrets never stay buried...

When revealed, Gabe realizes Lena's secrets are deeper than he ever imagined. For a man of his character, deception and lies of omission aren't negotiable. Will he be able to forgive the deceit? Or is the damage too great to ever repair?

Survivor Pass – Book Five
Redemption Mountain – Historical Western Romance Series

He thought he'd found a quiet life...

Cash Coulter settled into a life far removed from his days of fighting for the South and crossing the country as a bounty hunter. Now a deputy sheriff, Cash wants nothing more than to buy some land, raise cattle, and build a simple life in the frontier town of Splendor, Montana. But his whole world shifts when his gaze lands on the most captivating woman he's ever seen. And the feeling appears to be mutual.

But nothing is as it seems...
Alison McGrath moved from her home in Kentucky to the rugged mountains of Montana for one reason—to find the man responsible for murdering her brother. Despite using a false identity to avoid any tie to her brother's name, the citizens of Splendor have no intention of sharing their knowledge about the bank robbery which killed her only sibling. Alison knows her circle of lies can't end well, and her growing for Cash threatens to weaken the revenge which drives her.

And the troubles are mounting...
There is danger surrounding them both—men who seek vengeance as a way to silence the past...by any means necessary.

Reclaiming Love – Book One, A Novella

Peregrine Bay – Contemporary Romance Series

Adam Monroe has seen his share of setbacks. Now he's back in Peregrine Bay, looking for a new life and second chance.

Julia Kerrigan's life rebounded after the sudden betrayal of the one man she ever loved. As president of a success real estate company, she's built a new life and future, pushing the painful past behind her.

Adam's reason for accepting the job as the town's new Police Chief can be explained in one word—Julia. He wants her back and will do whatever is necessary to achieve his goal, even knowing his biggest hurdle is the woman he still loves.

As they begin to reconnect, a terrible scandal breaks loose with Julia and Adam at the center. Will the threat to their lives and reputations destroy their fledgling romance? Can Adam identify and eliminate the danger to Julia before he's had a chance to reclaim her love?

Our Kind of Love – Book Two
Peregrine Bay – Contemporary Romance Series

Selena Kerrigan is content with a life filled with work and family, never feeling the need to take a chance on a relationship—until she steps into a social world inhabited by a man with dark hair and penetrating blue eyes. Eyes that are fixed on her.

Lincoln Caldwell is a man satisfied with his life. Transitioning from an enviable career as a Navy SEAL to becoming a successful entrepreneur, his days focus on growing his security firm, spending his nights with whomever he chooses. Committing to one woman isn't on the horizon—until a captivating woman with caramel eyes sends his personal life into a tailspin.

Believing her identity remains a secret, Selena returns to work, ready to forget about running away from the bed she never should have gone near. She's prepared to put the colossal error, as well as the man she'll never see again, behind her.

Too bad the object of her lapse in judgment doesn't feel the same.

Linc is good at tracking his targets, and Selena is now at the top of his list. It's amazing how a pair of sandals and only a first name can say so much.

As he pursues the woman he can't rid from his mind, a series of cyber-attacks hit his business, threatening its hard-won success. Worse, and unbeknownst to most, Linc harbors a secret— one with the potential to alter his life, along with those he's close to, in ways he could never imagine.

Our Kind of Love, Book Two in the Peregrine Bay Contemporary Romance series, is a full-length novel with an HEA and no cliffhanger.

Colin's Quest – Book One
MacLarens of Boundary Mountain – Historical Western Romance Series

For An Undying Love...

When Colin MacLaren headed west on a wagon train, he hoped to find adventure and perhaps a little danger in untamed California. He never expected to meet the girl he would love forever. He also never expected her to be the daughter of his family's age-old enemy, but Sarah was a MacGregor and the anger he anticipated soon became a reality. Her father would not be swayed, vehemently refusing to allow marriage to a MacLaren.

Time Has No Effect...

Forced apart for five years, Sarah never forgot Colin—nor did she give up on his promise to come for her. Carrying the brooch he gave her as proof of their secret betrothal, she scans the trail from California, waiting for Colin to claim her. Unfortunately, her father has other plans.

And Enemies Hold No Power.
Nothing can stop Colin from locating Sarah. Not outlaws, runaways, or miles of difficult trails. However, reuniting is only the beginning. Together they must find the courage to fight the men who would keep them apart—and conquer the challenge of uniting two independent hearts.

Find all of my books at:
http://www.shirleendavies.com/books.html

www.ingramcontent.com/pod-product-compliance
Lightning Source LLC
Chambersburg PA
CBHW060245210726
48292CB00002BA/449